Maggie's cheeks burned with shame

She'd come so close to losing control—and Adam knew it.

But pride made her hold his gaze and say with honeyed sarcasm, "Surely that's why they call you Mr. Irresistible. And why I'd rather keep our future meetings on a strictly business footing."

At last he said. "You're still holding what happened in Bermuda against me, aren't you?"

"It has some bearing—yes."

"Aren't you making a mountain out of a molehill?" he suggested. "I didn't try to seduce you, if you remember."

Maggie looked straight ahead, but his hand curved around her cheek and turned her face toward him as he asked shrewdly, "Would you have resisted me, if I had?"

Anne Weale and her husband live in a Spanish villa high above the Mediterranean. An active woman, Anne enjoys swimming, interior decorating and antique hunting. But most of all she loves traveling. Researching new romantic backgrounds, she has explored New England, Florida, Canada, Australia, Italy, the Caribbean and the Pacific.

Books by Anne Weale

HARLEQUIN PRESENTS

HARLEQUIN ROMANCE

Don't miss any of our special offers. Write to us at the following address for information on our newest releases.

Harlequin Reader Service
901 Fuhrmann Blvd., P.O. Box 1397, Buffalo, NY 14240
Canadian address: P.O. Box 603,
Fort Erie, Ont. L2A 5X3

ANNE WEALE

do you remember babylon?

Harlequin Books

TORONTO • NEW YORK • LONDON
AMSTERDAM • PARIS • SYDNEY • HAMBURG
STOCKHOLM • ATHENS • TOKYO • MILAN

Harlequin Presents first edition May 1990
ISBN 0-373-11270-X

Original hardcover edition published in 1989
by Mills & Boon Limited

CHAPTER ONE

HALF-WAY across the Atlantic, on the Concorde flight from London to Barbados, a blonde girl in a window-seat on the starboard side of the aircraft handed a folded-back copy of an expensive magazine to her travelling companion.

'That might interest you.'

Never normally seen in public without a pair of lightly tinted glasses screening his brilliant eyes, Adam Rocquaine—sometimes called Britain's answer to Charles Aznavour—took the offered magazine and started to read the article she had indicated.

Having read it, he flipped through the rest of the glossy, skipping most of the fashion section but, towards the end, paying close attention to a feature on interior decoration.

'Is it OK to tear this page out?' he asked.

'Yes... what is it you want?'

'This piece about Maggie Hornchurch. Ever heard of her?'

'Can't say I have... but I like that room,' she said, looking at the page he was ripping out of the magazine.

'So do I. I'll make some enquiries about her. Might get her to do up my new place.' He folded the shiny page and tucked it away in the inside pocket of his immaculate silk tweed blazer.

Adam Rocquaine was noted for the expensive excellence of his tailoring. Most of his clothes were made for him by Tommy Nutter, the Savile Row tailor who catered to aristocrats with pizazz. With his clothes, his grooming, his civilised manners, Adam Rocquaine had brought the old-fashioned term 'debonair' back into currency. Like the Spanish singing star, Julio Iglesias, Rocquaine appealed to women of all ages, from teenage rockers to the audience for formation dancing. Men didn't understand his fascination.

Basically it was the indefinable but instantly recognisable sex appeal which had made international stars of Rudolph Valentino, Gary Cooper, Paul Newman and Robert Redford.

In Adam Rocquaine's case, sex appeal was allied to a melodious tenor singing voice and a gift for writing romantic songs guaranteed to tug female heartstrings.

The stewardesses on Concorde were accustomed to waiting on famous, rich and important men, including most of the world's heart-throbs. Even so, they felt definitely envious of the blonde girl sipping champagne alongside six feet of long-limbed, broad-shouldered masculinity topped by the kind of face which, if not classically handsome, was a combination of features no woman was likely to forget—particularly if the humorous mouth, with a hint of sensuality in the full lower lip, had suddenly curved into a smile while Adam Rocquaine was looking at her.

The blonde girl was listed on the passenger inventory as Ms E Vazon and one of the stewardesses had heard Adam Rocquaine call her Elizabeth. Presumably she was his girlfriend. She was very decorative and the raincoat she had handed over to be hung up during the flight had a Giorgio Armani label in it. The outfit she was wearing was probably by the same Italian designer. She was just the sort of glamorous but intelligent-looking woman Adam Rocquaine might be expected to have in the background, for he managed to keep his private life a good deal more private than the marriages, divorces and liaisons of most of the big names in popular music.

Thigh-deep in the warm turquoise sea which lapped the powdered coral beach adjoining the Caribbean garden of her most important clients to date, Maggie Hornchurch was laughing.

A few minutes earlier she had been swimming in deeper water, as she did every day before lunch. Then, on her way back to the beach, she had paused to watch a gang of six small islanders trying to form a human pyramid.

For a second or two the topmost boy had managed to balance unsteadily on the shoulders of the two beneath him, a big grin splitting his face at the achievement of this feat. Then one of the others had wobbled and the whole precarious edifice had collapsed in a mêlée of black arms and legs and white foam, making Maggie laugh aloud, although the sound of her amusement was lost in the louder yells of the boys as they bobbed to the surface, buoyant as corks in a sea which had been their playground since infancy.

As she strolled back to her towel, her next to naked body beaded with drops of water which rolled down her skin like crystals, Maggie continued to smile, not only at the antics of the children but because this was a place where, surrounded by beauty, she felt a strong sense of well-being.

Arriving in Barbados a week ago, her skin then winter-pale, she had been careful not to burn in the hot Caribbean sun. Caution had paid off. She was beginning to turn a becoming light golden brown, except where her pale blue bikini partially covered the rounded parts of her figure.

Maggie would have liked to have riper curves, but her metabolism and the demands of her work conspired against her ever developing a more voluptuous figure. With her hair a tousled mop of wet reddish-brown curls, and no make-up on her face, she looked about eighteen years old. In fact she was twenty-five, with six years of earning a living behind her.

It was luck as much as talent, she knew, which had brought her to this point in her career. After an unpromising start in life with incompatible parents who had eventually split up, from the moment she had left school luck had been with her all the way. Now interiors 'by Maggie Hornchurch' were appearing with increasing frequency in *House & Garden* and similar periodicals. Her own flat and a house for a client had been photographed for *The World of Interiors* and, with her current commission, she hoped to make *Town & Country*, the glossy read by top people in America.

If things continued to go as well for her in the next few years as they had in the past six, she could hope by the time she was thirty to be one of the top twenty international designers.

Whether by then she would also have achieved her other ambition was rather less certain, if not doubtful. For Maggie had a secret dream of not always living in London and being the archetypal career girl, working fourteen hours a day, seven days a week. She hoped that, some time in the future, her present life-style, absorbing though it was, would expand to include weekends at a large family house in the country, and children, and, above all, a husband.

Strangely, being the child of a broken marriage which had given her two step-parents, who had subsequently become ex-step-parents, hadn't put her off marriage. The behaviour of her father and mother and their other partners had been merely an object lesson in what to avoid if one wished to stay married. Maggie had a very clear picture of the man with whom she could settle down and live for the rest of her life. Until he showed up—if he ever did—she preferred to avoid any less serious relationships and concentrate on her work.

Leaving the beach where she swam and sunbathed early in the morning and late in the afternoon, with another swim but no sunbathe during her lunch break, Maggie strolled through the beautiful garden tended by a Barbadian gardener whose wife looked after the interior of Content.

Jim and Ella had been at Content for thirty years, during which time the house had had several owners, the most recent being a British tycoon and his wife. Having plenty of money but no confidence in their own taste, they had chosen Maggie to redecorate the house for them. Although not sure what they did want—which made them the most difficult type of clients—they were definite in their dislike of the previous occupants' furniture and decorations.

As Maggie mounted the steps to the wide veranda which surrounded three sides of the building, the housekeeper appeared.

'Telephone call for you, Mis' Maggie. From your office in London. They want you to call back. It's important, the young lady said.'

'Thanks, Ella. I'll do it right away.'

Maggie ran up the wide staircase and entered the much cooler atmosphere of the bedroom she was occupying. The main reception-rooms had ceiling fans, but all the bedrooms were air-conditioned and, although she didn't mind the heat and humidity of the Caribbean during the day, she was glad of a lower temperature at night.

In the adjoining bathroom she took off her bikini and dropped it in the bath to rinse when she had a shower. Then, wrapped in a dry towel, she went back to the bedroom to sit on the side of the bed and dial London, where the working day of her chief assistant, Alice Dulford, would be just beginning.

It didn't take long to get through. 'Hello, Alice. It's Maggie. What's up?'

'Oh, hi, Maggie. You'll never guess who's left a message on the machine.' The normally calm, un-flappable Alice sounded excited. 'Adam Rocquaine. He wants you to contact him immediately.'

For a second or two the name rang no bell in Maggie's mind. Listening to the radio or to records was some-thing she had no time for, and she rarely watched tele-vision unless a programme had some bearing on her work. But even though she had never felt moved to buy one of his albums, she had heard and liked some of the love songs of Adam Rocquaine, and it didn't take her long to place him.

'You'd better call and explain where I am at the moment,' she told Alice, '…also find out what he wants.'

'If the number he left was in England, I'd have done that, but it has the same code as yours…010 1 809. He must be in Barbados. The rest of the number is——' Alice read it out.

Having jotted down both code and number, Maggie said, 'Could this be a practical joke? Who dictated the message? Someone claiming to be his secretary?'

'No, it's his own voice. I would have recognised it even if he hadn't given his name. His speaking voice is as distinctive as his singing,' said her assistant.

'Distinctive voices are the easiest to imitate. I think it's some kind of leg-pull. But as it's a Barbados number I'll call it. Anything else of interest on the machine?' asked Maggie.

'No, only routine stuff. Lucky you...if it is Adam Rocquaine. I'd give my eye-teeth to meet him,' Alice said wistfully.

Maggie laughed and said goodbye. Then she dialled the number on the pad. She had reached the conclusion that there was no one there and was on the point of replacing the receiver when the ringing stopped and a somewhat breathless female voice said, 'Hello?'

'I have a message to call Mr Rocquaine.' Expecting to be told that she must have the wrong number, Maggie was surprised to hear that Mr Rocquaine was out to lunch.

'In that case would you ask him to call me when he comes in, please?' Maggie gave her name and number.

Standing under the shower, rinsing the salt water out of her hair, she wondered if the singer had bought himself a house on the island and wanted it refurbished. But, if so, why approach her? She had never had a showbiz client and, from what she had seen of pop stars' houses in magazines, didn't particularly want one. She hadn't yet reached the point when she could afford to turn down lucrative commissions. At the same time, she was reluctant to work for anyone with whom she felt no rapport. Although he made Alice drool, Maggie thought it unlikely Adam Rocquaine would have the same effect on her.

After a light salad lunch, prepared and served by Ella, Maggie went back to work until it was time for her third swim of the day.

Before going into the water she spent twenty minutes lying on her tummy, reading, to tan the backs of her legs, and then put her book aside and lay on her back, her head pillowed on one arm while her other hand sifted the pale pink powdered coral sand.

She had closed her eyes and was thinking how lucky she was to be here in this golden climate instead of enduring the worst of the winter in England when a male voice said, 'Hello.'

During her first days in Barbados, several beach boys had tried to chat her up. Politely but firmly she had discouraged their attentions, and now they no longer bothered her.

So it was with surprise that she opened her eyes and sat up to make it clear, yet again, that she hadn't come to the island for a holiday fling.

The man standing on the fine sand, two yards from her woven grass beach mat, was not a Barbadian. At first glance it was hard to tell where he came from. His height, the breadth of his shoulders and his fresh-from-the-shower look suggested he might be American, or possibly Canadian. But the cut of his taupe linen beach shirt and white shorts, and the blue canvas deck shoes dangling from one long lean hand, had an understated style which Maggie associated with Frenchmen and Italians. The one word he had spoken gave no clue to his origins. 'Hello' was a universal opener and, her thoughts elsewhere, she hadn't noticed his accent.

'Are you Maggie Hornchurch?' he asked, at the same time removing his sunglasses.

With his eyes—the colour of lapis lazuli—no longer masked by light-reactive lenses, there was no mistaking the face once pointed out to her by Alice in a window display made up entirely of sleeves of a new Adam Rocquaine album.

At the time she had thought that such brilliantly blue eyes must be a trick of lighting or colour printing. Now she saw that the sleeve hadn't exaggerated the dark, vivid colour of his irises. And the way he was looking down at her now was the same way he had looked at the camera which had taken that picture—gazing intently into the lens so that, even in a photograph, he had seemed to be making strong eye-contact.

The effect, in reality, was oddly mesmeric and disturbing. Maggie, who had once been rather shy but had trained herself to appear unfailingly self-possessed, even though it was sometimes an effort, experienced a sudden reversion to the gaucherie of her teens.

'Yes, I am,' she said. 'Who are you?'

If it surprised him not to be instantly recognised by a member of the sex over whom he exerted such a powerful influence, he didn't show it.

'I'm Adam Rocquaine. You called me earlier today. The housekeeper knew the number of this house'—he gestured towards Content—'and told me it wasn't far from the place I'm renting. I thought, rather than calling back, I'd stroll over and meet you.'

Maggie scrambled to her feet, quickly swathing herself in a kanga of sea-green cotton. Why she felt a need to cover up, she wasn't sure. But she did.

'How do you do, Mr Rocquaine.' She offered him her hand.

'How do you do.' His much larger hand enveloped hers in a clasp which was strong without being thoughtlessly painful to her more delicate bones. 'It's a stroke of luck that you're here at the same time as I am. Are you on holiday?'

'No, I'm working. The owners of Content want the whole interior redesigned. At the moment I'm here for two weeks.'

'That's great. It gives us plenty of time to talk over a project I'd like you to tackle for me.' Still holding her hand, he smiled at her.

Men often smiled at Maggie. Although neither a beauty nor an overtly sexy girl, she had something about her which made men of all ages nice to her. More than once, using the Underground between the West End and the Barbican at busy times of day, she had actually had seats offered to her—a rare and signal gallantry not experienced by many women.

But none of the men who had been pleasant to her, or tried to flirt with her, had ever evoked the reaction caused by Adam Rocquaine's smile. For the first time in her life she knew herself to be inside the magnetic field of a powerful physical attraction and her instinct was to leap back, putting herself outside the range of his dangerously disturbing aura.

Modified by her brain into acceptable social behaviour, that instinct emerged as the firm withdrawal of her hand and a rather cool tone of voice as she said, 'How did you come to hear of me, Mr Rocquaine?'

'Call me Adam. Everyone does. May I use your first name? Formality seems inappropriate when we're both barefoot.'

He glanced down at her slim brown feet, the toenails painted pearl pink. Automatically Maggie looked at his feet, which were equally tanned. Perhaps he had been on the island for some time, or perhaps he led the kind of life which gave him a tan all year round. Either way, his long legs were several shades darker than hers. But as he had black hair and eyebrows and she had a touch of the redhead in her colouring, even untouched by the sun, his skin would be darker than hers.

'I've seen photographs of your work which make me think you'd do a good job on an old village house I've bought. The structure needs restoration, so it isn't ready to decorate yet. Do you have a dinner date tonight?'

The question, tacked on unexpectedly, surprised her into saying, 'No.'

'Then have dinner with me and I'll tell you all about it. I've discovered a great little place to eat. It's not at all smart, but the food's good and I think you'll like the atmosphere. I'll pick you up at seven . . . OK?'

Taking her assent for granted, he gave her another of those heart-turning smiles and walked off along the beach, his shoulders looking even broader from the rear, his thighs and calves showing the muscles of a man who took hard and regular exercise.

For about half a minute Maggie stood gazing after him, not sure whether to be annoyed or to laugh. Then, unwinding the kanga, she dropped it on top of her mat and walked down the gentle slope to wade into the clear, warm water.

At five minutes to seven, waiting for Adam to fetch her, she still hadn't decided whether she liked or disliked him.

What was there to dislike about him? the voice of her reason enquired. Nothing in particular—as yet, conceded her instinctive self. Although hadn't there been a touch of arrogance in his assumption that, having no other date, she would be delighted to dine with him? Perhaps not. Perhaps his only assumption had been that any businesswoman would be pleased to dine with a prospective client. If and when he became an actual client, it was going to be important to distinguish between her personal and professional reactions to him.

At precisely one minute to seven he arrived, driving one of the canvas-canopied mokes which most tourists rented for transport around the island.

'Would you care for a drink?' she asked, when he stepped on to the veranda where she had been slowly sipping a tall glass of iced water.

'Thanks. A beer, if you have it. Are you alone here?'

'Except for Ella and Jim who run the place—yes. The owners are spending most of this winter in Florida. They'll be coming over from time to time to see how things are going.'

As she led him into the house, Ella appeared. Maggie introduced them and asked the housekeeper to bring a glass of lager to what was known as the Ocean Room.

'And another glass of water for me, please, Ella.'

'Don't you drink alcohol, Maggie?' Adam asked.

'Sometimes. Not very often. Wine makes me drowsy. Spirits give me a headache. I get my lifts from fruit juice,' she said, with a smile.

'Probably that's part of the reason why you look so much younger than I think you must be for a magazine to describe you as "one of the few women interior designers to be establishing herself in the same league as..." I've forgotten the names of the designers they mentioned.'

'Stefanidis, Mlinaric and Roos,' said Maggie, having read with incredulous pleasure the article about herself which had also come to his notice. To find herself compared to three designers she particularly admired, when the magazine had come out on her last day in London, had been a tremendous boost. She wondered if other clients would come her way as a result of it.

By now they had entered the Ocean Room with its view of the placid sea on the leeward side of the island.

'Good heavens! How *not* to do it,' was the singer's immediate exclamation, as he looked at the furnishings chosen by the present owners' predecessors.

'Yes, it is a bit . . . flamboyant,' Maggie said mildly, remembering her own recoil the first time she saw the gilded furniture upholstered with leopard-print velvet and scattered with gold lamé cushions.

'That's the understatement of the year.' He walked to the windows overlooking the beach. 'I find this so-called Platinum Coast less interesting scenically than the wilder Atlantic coast. Have you seen the other side of the island?'

She shook her head.

'You musn't miss it. It's the side where the locals have their holiday houses . . . away from the tourist areas. The visitors go to look but not to stay. The sea is too wild for swimming and jet-skiing.'

Ella came in with their drinks.

'If you's goin' to be out late, Mis' Maggie, maybe you'd like your breakfast later in the mornin'?' she suggested.

'I'll be up at my usual time, Ella. I've too much to do to sleep late like the tourists,' said Maggie. 'Anyway, early morning is the best time of day here,' she added, when Ella had left the room. 'Or are you a night owl, Mr Rocquaine?'

Although not normally a formal person, she felt, with this man, a need to keep him at arm's length.

'Not by nature, no. But sometimes my job obliges me to keep late hours. The night has its pleasures, too. Have you noticed the stars here?'

Again Maggie had to shake her head. 'Are you an amateur astronomer?'

'No, just an ordinary star-gazer...when there's a clear sky.'

His reply rang a bell. 'Isn't one of your songs about star-gazing? One of my assistants buys all your records as soon as they come out. She's among your greatest fans.'

'That's nice to hear.' A glint of sardonic amusement lit his extraordinary blue eyes. 'But they don't include you...am I right?'

Slightly embarrassed by his directness, she gave a small shrug and said, 'I'm a visual rather than an aural person. Most people are one or the other...not often both, don't you think?'

He drank some beer and considered the question. He wasn't at all like her idea of a top recording star. Allied to his physical magnetism, there was an authority about him which surprised her. He looked, she thought, like a man accustomed to responsibility...a pilot, or the skipper of a yacht.

'You could be right, but I think we should try to make full use of all our senses,' he answered. 'If one's work depends mainly on sight rather than sound, don't you think it's a good thing to develop the other senses out of working time? For instance, I get a lot of pleasure from looking at art and nature...and from my palate. Do you like eating, Maggie?'

As he asked the question, his eyes scanned her slender shape in the cool dress of fine white handkerchief lawn, exquisitely tucked and embroidered, she had found in an antique shop on one of her forays in search of the unusual and decorative pieces which were a hallmark of her style.

Wondering if he thought her too thin, she said, 'Yes, very much...and cooking. That's one thing I do make time for. Otherwise I have to admit I'm rather a work-aholic and don't have many outside interests. It's a matter of time. I just don't have enough time to run my business properly and do other things as well. Presumably the business side of your life is organised by other people?'

'To some extent, yes. Although I avoid supporting too many hangers-on.' He finished his beer. 'Shall we go? Are you mosquito-proofed?'

'Yes...Ella warned me about them and gave me some stuff to rub on my arms and legs.'

'What about a scarf for your hair? It can be blowy in the moke. I don't want to ruin your hairdo.'

She laughed. 'My hairdo took fifteen minutes after my shower. It will survive a few breezes. If necessary, I'll comb it when we get there.'

Opening the front door for her, he said, 'I've put clean beach towels over the seats, but be careful getting in. I don't think there are any smears of the last hirers' sun oil, but I can't guarantee it. These mokes are mainly for trips to the beach.'

She furled her full skirt and bounced lightly into the passenger seat, swinging her legs up and over the edge of the vehicle. His concern for her hair and her dress suggested that most of his female companions were much more fussy about their appearance than she was. But her wardrobe didn't include many expensive designer clothes, and she never went to a hairdresser except to have her curls cut.

Adam himself was wearing white trousers and a short-sleeved cotton shirt finely striped in pale blue, violet and khaki, colours which told her it was expensive. He wore no jewellery, she noticed, not even a signet ring, and his watch wasn't one of the status symbol makes but an ordinary, serviceable model on a scrubbable canvas strap. Glancing down, while they were still in the well-lit driveway, she saw that white buckskin loafers, worn without socks, completed his casual yet subtly stylish appearance.

Visually, she could find no fault with him. Clean nails. Unstyled but glossy-clean hair, neither too long nor too short. A pleasant aroma of soap and aftershave, and no trace of nicotine on his breath or fingers; he seemed to exemplify all her personal likes and none of her dislikes.

But what of the man inside the personable exterior? Was his appeal only skin-deep, or was he likeable all through? Perhaps by the time he brought her back she would have a clearer idea of whether she wanted to enter the prolonged association which a designer's relationship with a private client usually involved.

The drive to their destination didn't take long. After passing the spotlit gateways to several of the luxury hotels, Adam turned the moke down a lane on the seaward side of the coast road. A few minutes later he parked it alongside some other vehicles at the back of what appeared to be a timber-built shack with a corrugated iron roof.

By the time he came round to help her, Maggie had hopped out unaided and was shaking out her skirt. She could hear West Indian music, but thought it was probably a disc rather than a live group which was filling the night with the sound of a steel band.

Adam took hold of her arm, just above the elbow, and steered her through a gap in a hedge and along a planked walkway which led to a large timber platform with some of its supports in the sea and some embedded in the sand of a tiny beach.

On the platform were about eight tables spread with bright plastic cloths and lit by candles and loops of coloured lights strung among the rafters of a palm-thatched roof. Savoury cooking smells and the sizzle of hot fat issued from inside the shack where an enormously stout Barbadian woman could be glimpsed cooking.

It was only when they were seated at a table above the sea that Maggie realised Adam had slipped on a pair of dark glasses and chosen to sit with his back to the other people there, not all of them tourists.

'Sorry about the shades, but it cuts down the chance of being recognised, which I try to avoid on holiday,' he said. 'I wouldn't advise drinking the water here. How about Coke with a dash of rum in it?'

When the drinks and food had been ordered, Maggie felt it was time to start talking business.

'Where is the house you want decorated?' she asked, hoping it wouldn't be too far outside London. She had a driving licence but no car. So far one hadn't been necessary. She had managed with public transport and occasional rented cars.

'It's in a village in Spain.'

'In Spain?' Maggie's surprise was mixed with disappointment. She associated Spain with overcrowded beaches, high-rise hotels and, in the south, colonies of expatriates, some of whom were no longer welcome in their own countries.

Her unfavourable impression must have shown in her face. Adam said, 'Not in the tourist belt. My house is among the mountains in Catalonia which, in medieval times, was a kingdom stretching into France.'

That certainly sounded more promising. 'Is it near the Pyrenees? Is skiing the attraction?'

It was easy to imagine him on skis, skimming down a difficult piste, his eyes masked by snow goggles, his long frame perfectly balanced on the hissing blades.

'No, it's a long way from Andorra, which is the main skiing centre. The attraction of Pobla de Cabres is that it's well off the beaten track in a part of Spain which hasn't been spoiled by tourism. In fact, the village is so remote that the Catalans themselves have deserted it.'

At this point one of the two smiling teenage waitresses—perhaps the daughters of the ample woman in the kitchen—brought bowls of chilled cucumber soup sprinkled with chives.

'I first heard about the village while I was on holiday on a small island off Antigua last winter,' Adam continued. 'The Palm Reef Club and Pobla de Cabres are both owned by a man called Oliver Thornham whose wife, incidentally, is a dress designer...Laurian.'

Maggie's interest quickened. The year before she had invested in a beautifully cut and finished suit by Laurian, and there was a chestnut silk shirt by the designer in the current issue of *Vogue* which tempted her to splurge again.

'Thornham's idea is to make the village a retreat for people, who live in the limelight and sometimes need to escape from it, or for people who need a quiet retreat,' Adam went on. 'He's commissioned a Spanish architect to restore and modernise the houses, and already more than half have been sold, although they haven't been advertised. Thornham himself is vetting all prospective buyers. Anyone he doesn't like will be diplomatically turned down.' His smile gave a glimpse of white teeth, but not the unnaturally regular teeth of expensive cosmetic dentistry. 'Fortunately I passed muster.'

'If most of the residents are going to be celebrities, won't that attract attention from the press and the public?' she suggested.

'We hope not. Although it's only three hours' drive from Barcelona airport, which makes it conveniently accessible from London and other European capitals, the village is too far away from the major Spanish resorts to attract coachloads of sightseers. Thornham doesn't want it to be the kind of fenced-in, security-guarded enclave in which some of the rich and famous take refuge. None of his selected residents will be people who go in for conspicuous extravagance, and the village won't be the scene of wild parties or any other newsworthy activities,' he said drily.

The soup was followed by baked flying-fish pie with a golden crust of sliced yams.

'In most restaurants they use any old white fish, but here, so I'm told, it really is fresh flying-fish bought direct from the fishermen on the Atlantic coast,' he told her.

'Tell me about your house,' said Maggie, striving to keep her mind on the reason for this dinner *à deux* and finding it a little difficult in this romantic setting, with the sea glittering in the moonlight and the most attractive man she had ever met on the other side of the table.

'It's three cottages knocked into one. They're part of a terrace in a very steep street, so all the rooms will be on different levels. The ones with the best views of the surrounding mountains are on the top floors, so I want them made into a rambling living-room with the bedrooms below.'

'Will you be doing any work there? Or only relaxing?'

Being a dedicated careerist herself, who never went anywhere without a sketch-pad and pencil, her first thought had been that he would need a piano. Which might be a problem to install in a house with the sort of openings and stairways which peasants' dwellings usually had.

'I'm hoping to do a lot of work there. In fact, if the place develops in the way Thornham plans, I may even make it my main home. The winter climate is cooler than in the extreme south of Spain, but it's significantly warmer than where I live now...in Guernsey.'

Maggie had assumed that he lived either in London or not far outside it, perhaps in some fashionable part of the Thames valley inhabited by other pop stars and TV personalities.

'I've never been to the Channel Islands. Have you lived there long?' she asked.

'I was born and bred there, like generations of Rocquaines before me. One exception was my father. With World War Two imminent, he was sent to an English public school before Hitler's forces occupied the islands. He married an English girl, became a diplomat and spent most of his life abroad. I was a day boy at Elizabeth College in St Peter Port, and spent most of the holidays in Guernsey with my widowed grandmother. A few years ago I inherited her house. What about you? Where are your roots?'

'In Charterhouse Square, in the East End of London, where I live and have my office,' she said. 'As a child, my roots were at school. My parents divorced and remarried; in my mother's case, twice. My father and both my stepfathers are men who don't stay put, so I spent my school holidays all over the place.'

'Has that made you a nomad yourself, or had the opposite effect?'

Surprised that she had confided the facts of her childhood to him, Maggie said, 'I'm not sure. I sometimes think——' She stopped short, changing what she had been going to say to, 'Have you any ideas about how you want your place in Spain furnished?'

He didn't press her to complete the aborted remark, but said, 'I know what I don't want. I'm not at all keen on the heavy, dark, Spanish Inquisition style of furniture which a lot of foreigners in Spain go in for. Nor am I much impressed by the modern stuff available locally. My grandmother's house is crammed with island-made antiques. I'll probably take some of those down. If you're prepared to tackle the Pobla de Cabres house for me, you could come over to Guernsey and help me choose suitable pieces.'

An old house crammed with old things was Maggie's idea of heaven, and she envied him the security of growing up under his grandmother's wing in a small sea-girt community where probably, then if not still, the pace of life was much slower and more relaxed than on the mainland.

Instead of expressing these thoughts, she said, 'When are the renovations due to be finished? And how soon after that do you want the house to be habitable?'

'The builders should have finished by the end of next month, but the decoration doesn't have to be finished by any set date. I'm not planning to invite any friends to stay with me in Spain this summer. If the weather is good, I'll spend most of it in Guernsey... when I'm not away on tour. Could you get it done by next autumn? Say the first of October?'

'Possibly,' she said cautiously, knowing that projects abroad were seldom as straightforward as those undertaken in England, where she had a reliable task force of tradesmen to turn to. In Spain, as here in Barbados, she would have to spend time finding out where those skills were to be found.

'But I think you're being a bit precipitate...offering the job to me on the strength of seeing a few photographs. You ought to have a look at some actual schemes before committing yourself...and I think I should see the house and perhaps talk to Mr Thornham or his architect. Does he speak English?'

'Excellent English,' said Adam. 'And he's married to an English girl who is also bilingual. His name is Diego Montfalcó and hers is Lucinda. They'll both be living in the village until the whole scheme is completed. Diego's from Barcelona, but she knows the region round Pobla de Cabres well and she's going to help any wives of owners who want to choose the decorations themselves. Not having a wife, I need professional assistance.'

She wondered if he had ever had a wife. He looked about thirty, so perhaps there was a marriage which hadn't lasted in his past. She found herself hoping there wasn't.

The second waitress, her black hair dressed in the style known as corn rows, came to clear away their plates. Glass dishes of ice-cream were brought by the first girl.

'Two more rum and Cokes, please,' said Adam. 'I don't think the coffee here is likely to be up to much,' he added, when she was out of earshot. 'Probably made with condensed milk, which I don't like, do you?'

'No, but we could ask for it black. It would help to counterbalance the rather lavish measures of rum they dole out,' she said, hoping a second strong rum and Coke wouldn't go to her head.

He seemed to sense the concern underlying her remark, but misunderstood it. 'Don't worry. I know my limits. You'll arrive home in one piece. I thought we might run up the coast as far as the end of your beach and I'll walk you back to the house. Beach-walking at night is good when there's a full moon, but I wouldn't recommend it for a woman on her own.'

Having a tantalising view of the beach from the bedroom she was using, Maggie had already contemplated strolling by the water's edge after her solitary evening meal. But Ella had warned her against it, and against swimming at night. The majority of the islanders were friendly and helpful to visitors. But, as in resorts everywhere, there was a minority element which resented the tourists and, as Adam had just implied, a woman on her own was always at risk.

'The Americans renting the house next door to Content had a barbecue on the beach the other night,' she told him. 'I was tempted to gatecrash. There's a big family party staying there, including grandparents and babies.'

'If they had known you were alone, they'd have invited you along,' he said. 'Americans are far more hospitable than Europeans, I find. Have you been to America?'

'Not yet. I suppose you've been many times?'

'Yes, but always on tour, with not enough time to see the places which interest me most. The stamps in my passport give a misleading impression that I'm widely travelled. Which I am, in a sense. I've flown round the world several times and stayed in most of the big cities, but one hotel room is pretty much like another, whether it's in Sydney, Vancouver or Tokyo. These islands in the

Caribbean, where I take a break every winter, are the places I know best. Where do you go for your holidays?'

'I enjoy working so much that I don't need proper holidays. This trip to Barbados is as much of a break as I need—with the added advantage that it isn't costing me anything. You do realise that using an English designer is going to be much more expensive than having a Spanish one because of the travelling expenses?'

'Yes, I'm prepared for that.' His tone was amused. 'If you're thinking I must be either hard up or tight-fisted to have brought you here rather than to one of the smart places, you're wrong. I don't care for the jet-set ambience. I find this sort of place more fun.'

'That wasn't at all what I was thinking,' said Maggie. 'I expect you're extremely rich, but that doesn't mean you want to waste money. I remember the late Paul Getty telling an interviewer that, although he was a multi-millionaire, he wouldn't pay through the nose for anything. Most of my clients are rich people, but I try to spend their money as carefully as if it were mine.'

Her fingers were loosely curled round the base of her tall glass. To her surprise, he put his hand over her wrist and gave it a gentle squeeze.

'I'm sure you do, Maggie. Having spent a couple of hours with you, I'm sure any work you undertake will be given maximum attention at minimum expense. Life has made me wary of trusting people...but I'd trust you.'

As he spoke, he pushed his dark glasses down the high bridge of his nose, revealing his lazuli eyes, their expression as serious as his tone. For a moment her startled gaze was locked with his. Then Adam removed his hand, replaced the mask of dark glass and turned to beckon the waitress.

By the time he had ordered black coffee, Maggie had recovered her self-possession and was able to carry on the conversation as if nothing untoward had happened. But, as they continued talking, a part of her mind was uneasily aware not only that she was attracted to him, but that she could very easily become infatuated with him—like the hundreds of thousands of fans who had never met him in the flesh and felt the full impact of his charm.

As they were leaving Bella's Place, as the establishment was called, Adam put his head and shoulders through the door of the shack to tell Bella they had enjoyed her cooking and would be coming again.

Walking back to the moke, Maggie knew it would be sensible to find some excuse to avoid the beach-walk. But, although her common sense warned her to keep their relationship on a strictly businesslike footing, there were other forces at work in her and they proved the stronger.

'Do you think the beach towels might disappear in your absence?' she said, when he had parked the car at the north end of the long strand of moon-blanched sand which fronted the grounds of Content and several other handsome old houses.

'I'll lock them up.' He folded the towels and stowed them in the moke's small locker. 'And my shoes with them.'

While Maggie was taking off her sandals, he turned up the bottoms of his trousers which, having straight legs, could be folded up to the muscular swell of his calves.

'Let me carry your shoes for you. Don't worry, I shan't drop them in the water.' He took them from her.

At first sight the beach seemed deserted, until the red glow of a cigarette end in the shadow of a sea-grape caught her eye and she saw someone sitting there, his dark skin and clothing making him almost invisible.

Adam saw him too, and lifted a hand in greeting, but the gesture wasn't acknowledged.

'May not be feeling sociable or may be "high",' he murmured to her.

Maggie knew that, on her own, she would have been nervous of the motionless figure watching her pass. With Adam beside her, she felt protected and safe.

Paddling happily through the lukewarm shallows, looking towards the white line of surf which indicated the presence of a submerged reef of coral, she said, 'Are you going back to Guernsey when you leave here?'

'No, I'll be in London for a week. So will the Thornhams. I'll arrange for the four of us to get together. You and Laurian will have a lot in common, even though you work in different fields.'

'I'd like to meet her very much.'

As they neared the grounds of Content, he said, 'We were talking about star-gazing earlier. This is the best way to do it.' Leaving the shallows, he first sat down on the dry sand and then lay back at full length, using one arm as a headrest. 'Come and try it.'

On visits to Italy and France, while she was a student, Maggie had seen a few people lying on the floors of churches and palaces, the better to admire ceilings painted by old masters. There seemed no reason to jib at lying down here for a few minutes to view one of nature's most beautiful spectacles.

'Wait a minute...have this under your head.' Adam sat up and produced a folded handkerchief which he shook out and spread on the sand beside him.

Had it not been for this chivalrous action, she would have lain down a couple of metres away from him. But he had left her no choice but to lie beside him, as close as if they were sharing a double bed.

At the thought of being in a bed with him, she found herself trembling inwardly, her heart pounding inside her chest.

Striving to concentrate on the stars and not to be foolishly disturbed by the proximity of the long masculine frame stretched alongside her, she said, hoping her voice sounded normal, 'What is that very bright star almost directly overhead?'

Adam named the star and explained that, being near the equator, they could see stars in both hemispheres; about two thousand of them with the naked eye, more with a pair of binoculars.

While he was explaining about constellations and magnitudes, Maggie tried to pay intelligent attention. It wasn't easy when the night was so beautiful and she was lying close to a man who was a world-class heart-throb, and not only that but a very nice person as well. One of the nicest men she had ever met.

No, not merely one of—*the* nicest.

What shall I do if he kisses me? she wondered. What if he invites himself in for a nightcap? What if he tries to stay the night? Probably he knows that Jim and Ella have their own quarters away from the main part of the house. They won't know if I let him stay. Not if he leaves at first light.

There was a movement beside her: Adam rising from the sand with one cat-supple upward flow of his tall, limber frame. As he held out both hands to help her up, she wouldn't have been surprised to find herself drawn into his arms.

But it wasn't until they were at Content's garden gate, where a shade tree made a pool of darkness in the bright tropical night, that he turned her towards him with light but sure hands on her shoulders.

An instant later his lips were gentle on her cheek; and then, all at once, firm and sure like his hands, on her mouth.

'Mornin', Mis' Maggie. Did you have a nice time last night?'

The housekeeper hadn't finished setting the table on the veranda outside the Ocean Room when Maggie returned from her early swim.

'Good morning, Ella. Yes, thank you...very nice. We had flying-fish pie at Bella's Place.'

'Is that so?' Ella seemed surprised. 'I made sure an important man like Mr Rocquaine would have taken you somewhere swish like Sandy Lane or the Casuarina Club. I hear tell he's a famous singer.'

Maggie nodded. 'And a songwriter. But he doesn't like to be recognised when he's on holiday, and he likes to go where the best food is—even if it isn't swish,' she added, smiling.

She had been smiling mentally, if not physically, ever since she woke up. Although it was rare for her to wake up feeling unenthusiastic about the day ahead, today she had known from the moment she opened her eyes that overnight her world had changed for the better.

'Is that so?' Ella said again. Then she pursed her lips and said 'Hmph!' in a rather odd way before going back to the kitchen.

For a moment Maggie was puzzled by something in the housekeeper's manner, but she had more important things to think about, such as when she would see Adam again. If she closed her eyes, she could still feel the light pressure of his parting kiss on her mouth.

'I'll call you,' he had murmured, his long fingers sliding softly over her cheek.

I have fallen in love, thought Maggie, in a daze of happiness. What I've always longed for has happened...at last I'm in love...with a total stranger whom I feel I have known all my life.

She was still in a trance of bliss when Ella returned with her breakfast.

'My friend Cornelia keeps house for the people who own the house Mr Rocquaine is renting for his vacation,' said the older woman as she transferred a dish of chopped fruit and a glass of orange juice from her tray to the table.

'Oh, really? So that's how you found out who he is?' said Maggie.

'Yes...and that's not all Cornelia told me.'

This time the undercurrent of meaning in the housekeeper's tone was too strong to be disregarded.

A very slight frisson of apprehension disturbed Maggie's joyous mood. 'What else did she tell you, Ella?'

'I don't want to bad-mouth no one, Mis' Maggie, but it's right you should know that Mr Rocquaine ain't come here on his own. There's a lady with him...a young lady...and she ain't family to him. They don't look nothing alike. Her hair's the colour of sweetcorn, and it don't come out of no bottle, Cornelia says.' Ella placed the milk jug alongside the coffee-pot. Then she looked Maggie in the eye. 'Did he tell you 'bout her, Mis' Maggie?'

The sun was warm on her bare back, but suddenly Maggie felt cold. 'No, he didn't,' she answered. 'But I don't think you quite understand the situation, Ella.

Having dinner with Mr Rocquaine was a business, not a social engagement. He wants me to decorate a house in Europe for him. I don't know why he didn't bring his friend with him last night, but a girlfriend isn't like a wife. He may not include her in everything he does.'

It surprised her that she could speak so calmly and casually, as if Ella's information were only of minor interest to her, not a bombshell which in one terrible instant had exploded her euphoria.

Mentally reeling from the shock, she reached for the glass of juice in an instinctive effort to behave as if nothing had happened.

'The young lady ain't been feelin' good these past few days,' said Ella. 'She's had a sick headache. Maybe the sun don't suit her. Anyways, she's been stayin' in her room with the curtains closed because the light hurts her eyes. I never had the migraine myself, but I hear it's a terrible bad pain and there ain't nothing much the doctors can do for it.'

'No, I believe not,' said Maggie. She glanced at her watch. 'I have an appointment at nine and I'll probably be out to lunch. If Mr Rocquaine should telephone, would you tell him I'm busy today and I'll call him when I have time.'

The housekeeper nodded. 'Sure thing.'

To Maggie's relief, she went away, the sound of her flip-flops growing fainter as she sauntered back to the kitchen. Ella never bustled. Already the coolness of early morning was over. From now until noon the temperature would rise until it was impossible to walk on the burning sand with bare feet. Any vigorous activity made people hot and sweaty, which was why the Barbadians didn't hurry themselves but went about their work at a pace which might seem lethargic to newcomers but was a necessary adaptation to the island's climate.

Left alone, Maggie put her elbows on the table and buried her face in her hands. For the first time in years she felt like venting her disappointment and chagrin in a burst of angry tears.

How could she have been such a fool as to think herself head over heels in love with a man who had only been playing with her? Probably he played the same game with every passable woman who came his way. He might not have meant any harm by it. He might have thought she understood that it was only a game, not to be taken seriously. It wasn't as if she were a gullible teenager. She was twenty-five years old, long past the age of being taken for a ride by a practised philanderer. Or so he would have been entitled to think. How was he to know that inside the successful careerwoman there was a romantic girl with next to no experience of relationships with the opposite sex because she had been too busy building a business—and also too afraid of being hurt?

There had been so many hurts during her childhood. At first, when her parents had split up, she had thought it was partly her fault. Now she knew that was a common reaction among children whose parents divorced, but knowing she had played no part in the breakdown of the marriage didn't blot out the anguish she had suffered while thinking herself to blame.

Later there had been other hurts. The discovery that her father's second wife found her an annoying reminder of the existence of his first wife. Then the even more painful realisation that her mother—always a man's woman—preferred the baby boy born shortly after her second marriage to her daughter by her first husband.

Looking back, Maggie could see that she had had the bad luck to have parents who were both too self-centred to be good at marriage or parenthood. There were many people born with worse misfortunes. But knowing that she shouldn't allow a poor start to become a permanent chip on her shoulder, and being grateful for the good luck which had given her a flair on which to found a career, hadn't cured her of the fear of being hurt again.

Only finding someone who loved her and didn't let her down would do that. Last night, between sunset and midnight, she had thought that person had materialised in the shape of Adam Rocquaine.

You fool! You consummate idiot! she berated herself. What made you imagine you were special enough to make him lose his heart to you? Those two rum and Cokes really did addle your wits, didn't they? If you'd been stone-cold sober you'd have known that he couldn't have fallen for you. He's probably beach-walked and star-gazed with dozens of girls, including the blonde who's staying with him. If she hadn't been unwell, he'd have taken her to Bella's Place. You thought him so considerate. Had he been the man you took him for, he would have stuck around while she was feeling rotten. Obviously all he considers is his own enjoyment.

Although she had lost her appetite, Maggie forced herself to eat her customary breakfast before going to her room to shower and dress for the day.

Her early appointment was to discuss some fitments she had designed with the man who was said to be the island's best cabinet-maker. Afterwards she went to see a girl who was making a name for herself with hand-printed textiles. They had lunch together which, in a different mood, Maggie would have enjoyed.

But the thought of Adam and how to face him, knowing what she knew now, lurked at the back of her mind all through the day.

Driving along lanes bordered by fields of tall sugar-cane in the ancient Daimler which belonged to Content, she had racked her brains for an acceptable reason for Adam's failure to disclose that he wasn't alone in Barbados. The very fact that he hadn't mentioned his companion affirmed the nature of their relationship.

Whether the blonde was in love with him, or was merely along for the ride, was something Maggie would never know. She hoped it was the latter. She felt sorry for anyone who loved him. Now, no longer under the influence of rum and Caribbean moonlight, she could see that an unattached man of thirty who was good-looking, rich and famous was very unlikely ever to settle for one woman. Why should he?

Men, it was said, weren't monogamous by nature. The reason many of them accepted monogamy was that they couldn't afford more than one partner. Given Adam's resources and opportunities, probably a majority would follow his example.

Ella was out when she returned to the house, but had left a note. Her assistant in London wanted Maggie to telephone her. Mr Rocquaine had called at Content during the morning and had said he would come back later.

Maggie dialled the number of her office. When she heard Alice's voice, she said, 'Maggie here. What's to do?'

'I'm dying of curiosity. Was the call from Adam Rocquaine bogus or genuine?'

Maggie hesitated. 'It was genuine . . . but you'll have to contain your curiosity for another day. I've decided to cut this trip short. I'm flying back tonight. You'll hear all about it tomorrow. See you in the morning.'

As she replaced the receiver, she wondered how, without disillusioning Alice, she was going to convince her that Adam Rocquaine wasn't a name she wanted to add to her list of clients.

CHAPTER TWO

AFTER checking that there was a seat for her on the flight to London, it didn't take Maggie long to pack. She made a point of travelling light, with all her vital belongings in a cabin bag so that if her suitcase went astray she wouldn't be seriously inconvenienced.

While she was packing, she worked out a way to avoid having to see Adam again. Although it would have given her a good deal of satisfaction to tell him to his face what she thought of him, she suspected that her own embarrassment would far outweigh his.

When Ella returned, Maggie said, 'I have to go back to London sooner than I expected. I'll be leaving tonight and I'll also be out to dinner. If Mr Rocquaine calls again, would you ask him to leave his address and say I'll be writing to him about his house in Spain? I've ordered a taxi to take me to the airport. There's no point in Jim turning out at that time of night.'

Without saying where she was going, but assuring Ella she would be back in good time, she took a towel and a swimsuit and drove to one of the hotels for a final bathe and somewhere to sit and read until it was safe to return to Content without risking a confrontation with the man she hoped never to set eyes on again.

Swimming from the hotel's beach, she thought how tiresome it was to have to curtail her trip like this, although it wouldn't disrupt her work in Barbados to any serious extent. She was confident that the craftsmen she had engaged would stick to the specifications she had given them. When she returned to put in hand the next phase, Adam and his blonde would be gone, and by then Maggie herself would have put last night out of her mind.

All the larger hotels in Barbados being open to non-residents, no one took any notice of her as she sat in a quiet corner of a lounge adjoining the reception area, sometimes trying to concentrate on her book, sometimes watching the comings and goings of the people staying there. When they started to filter into the hotel's dining-room, she beckoned a waiter wearing the hibiscus-patterned shirt which was the male staff's uniform, and ordered coffee and a sandwich to keep her going until dinner was served on the aeroplane.

She returned to Content in time to wash and dry her hair. As she had been swimming until the sun set, her suit was still damp but could travel in a plastic bag.

'Yes, Mr Rocquaine came by,' Ella told her. 'But he wouldn't leave no address. He said he'd be seeing you in London.'

Not if I can help it, thought Maggie.

When she arrived at the airport, it was already crowded with passengers for the British Airways flight. About two-thirds of them were white holidaymakers, some with small children who normally would have been in bed at this time of night and were fretful from tiredness.

The rest of the passengers were black or the shades of coffee-brown resulting from mixed ethnic origins. They had also been holidaying on the island, and now were being seen off by cheerful or tearful groups of Barbadian friends and relations.

Maggie was flying first class. It increased the expenses she charged to her clients, but it also cut down on travel fatigue and meant that she arrived with her energy un-drained by the hassle of tourist-class travel with not enough leg room or elbow room to work on their behalf in flight.

She was in the first-class lounge, discreetly surveying her few fellow passengers, and hoping the seat next to hers would be unoccupied as it had been on the outward flight, when the bored-looking girl she was watching suddenly perked up in the unmistakable manner of a female who has spotted some top-class male talent approaching.

Maggie swivelled her gaze towards the entrance to the lounge, expecting to see a young man in his early twenties coming in. When what she saw was Adam Rocquaine's tall figure, her heart gave a violent lurch.

He was having a word with the ground hostess on duty by the door, obviously explaining that he wasn't a pas-senger but had come to see someone who was. It was equally obvious that, even though she was used to famous faces, the hostess was reacting to his charismatic presence as strongly as if Sidney Poitier had just strolled in.

Maggie heard her say, 'Miss Hornchurch is over there, sir.'

The next moment Adam was advancing towards her. She was trapped. Not only that, by now everyone in the lounge seemed to have recognised that a VIP had ar-rived, and would be watching and straining to hear their conversation.

'I was sorry to hear you are having to rush back to London,' said Adam, seating himself in the chair next to hers. 'Ella said she didn't know the reason. It's not something unpleasant, I hope?'

'No, just something important which needs my immediate attention. What brings you to the airport?' she enquired coolly. 'Are you meeting an incoming flight?'

It would have been difficult to hang on to her composure had they been alone. Knowing they were now the cynosure of all the other first-class passengers made it even harder.

'I came to say goodbye to you. Or rather, *au revoir* until I follow you back.'

Adam removed his dark glasses, giving her the full impact of his forget-me-not-blue eyes.

Maggie mustered all her self-possession. 'I'm afraid it has to be goodbye. I've been reviewing my programme for the next twelve months and there's no way I can fit in another overseas commission. I'm sorry, but I won't be able to take on your house in Spain. Mine is still a small business, and there's a limit to how many jobs I can accept and do full justice to.'

Did he believe her? It was impossible to tell.

'I see,' he said. 'That's a pity. Last night you sounded as if you would be able to manage it.'

'I didn't have my diary with me. When I looked at it today, I realised I couldn't after all. If you like, I can post you the names of several designers who may be able to take it on and who'd do a very good job for you.'

'Are interior designers interchangeable? I should have thought it was like having a portrait painted. If one wants a John Ward, a John Bratby isn't a satisfactory substitute, or vice versa.'

Clearly he didn't intend to accept her decision gracefully. He was too used to having his own way, she thought vexedly. But at least she had the advantage that the flight would be called before long, and that would put an end to the discussion.

'It's not the same thing,' she answered. 'A painting by a great portraitist is always recognisable as his work. The hallmarks of good interior designers are much more subtle. They don't try to impose their own style on their clients. They attempt to crystallise the client's style. If I were you, I'd try David Mlinaric. He's advisor to the National Trust, but he might enjoy a complete change from historic houses. His own country house in Suffolk is beautifully done...very simple and rustic...exactly the sort of treatment your Spanish house needs, by the sound of it.'

'Perhaps...but I want you,' he said, and the way he looked at her mouth made it clear that he wasn't referring only to her professional help.

The amorous look, and her own response to it, made Maggie angry. What right had he to pursue her when he was already involved with another woman?

Deciding to make it clear that she knew the type of man he was, she said, 'Ella knows Cornelia, your housekeeper. I hear the friend you brought with you hasn't been well. How unfortunate. Is she still laid low?'

Surprise and something else—discomfiture?—showed in his lean, dark face for a second or two. 'It's not serious. She's improving.' After a pause, he added, 'Is that why you've changed your mind about doing my Spanish house?'

She had expected him to be quick at putting two and two together; but not that he would parry her oblique accusation in this direct fashion.

'No—but it did make it clear that you and I don't have the kind of rapport which makes for a good client-designer relationship,' she replied shortly.

His eyes narrowed, showing a gleam of mockery. 'Last night we seemed totally *en rapport*.'

An uncontrollable blush suffused Maggie's lightly tanned face. Her mouth, which a fellow art student had once told her reminded him of the lips of Botticelli's angels, compressed in a tight line. Her hazel eyes sparkled indignantly.

'Last night was an aberration which I very much regret,' she told him, keeping her voice low.

The lift of one mobile dark eyebrow indicated his scepticism. Then his expression altered, becoming colder and harder.

'Perhaps it was an aberration on my part too,' he said. 'Last night I took you for someone who would always take the charitable view, not assume the worst about people. If you had heard something off-putting, why didn't you ask me about it? You knew my telephone number.'

'I've been busy today. Are you saying my conclusion is wrong? That the girl with you isn't your girlfriend?'

At that moment it was announced that the passengers could take their seats on the aircraft.

As people began to put away their books and papers, and to gather their hand-baggage together, Adam said, 'There isn't time to discuss it...and I'm not sure you would understand if I tried to explain it to you. Goodbye, Maggie. *Bon voyage.*'

He rose to his feet and replaced his sunglasses, ignoring the interested glances which followed him as he strode from the lounge.

Usually Maggie managed to sleep well on night flights. She always changed into a long, loose houserobe and asked the stewardess to hang up the clothes in which she had boarded so that they wouldn't be crumpled when she landed.

On this flight, although she put on a sleep-mask and snuggled under the soft blanket offered by the stewardess, her thoughts wouldn't let her rest.

What would Adam have explained to her if she had rung up and asked him about the girl who was sharing the house with him?

When she had asked him point-blank if she had jumped to the wrong conclusion, he hadn't said yes. He hadn't denied the blonde *was* his girlfriend.

All night—or so it seemed—she went over and over their conversation at the airport. She remembered the look in his eyes when he said '... but I want *you*' and, a few minutes later, the finality of his 'Goodbye, Maggie.'

At last she fell into the heavy sleep of exhaustion, from which she was woken gently by the stewardess to find it was time for breakfast.

Low clouds were hanging over southern England as the aircraft approached Heathrow. When she had hoisted her suitcase off the carousel, Maggie pushed her trolley as far as the Underground ticket office and caught the tube to Holborn station where she took a taxi the rest of the way to her office.

This and the design studio were on the third floor of the building, with her flat and a store-room on the top floor. There was no lift, but Maggie and her small staff were all young and agile and thought nothing of running up and down the somewhat stark, prison-like stone stairs which gave no hint of the light, airy, elegant premises awaiting visitors at the top.

This morning, however, four flights seemed a long way to haul her case and her flight-bag, and she was not looking forward to the inevitable barrage of questions from Alice about Adam Rocquaine.

Having unpacked, she took a quick shower and put on a sweater and trousers. It felt strange to be back in winter clothes after her time in the sun, and the rain which had begun to spatter the windows did nothing to raise her spirits.

'You look terrific!' was Alice's greeting, when Maggie walked into the studio where her colleagues were at work, her tanned face and hands in marked contrast to their mid-winter pallor.

'Hi! How's it going?' said Maggie, assuming an air of cheerfulness.

She had never shared her personal problems with the others, although she listened sympathetically to theirs. Not that she'd had many problems, except those relating to work. With no private life to speak of, up to now she had escaped the emotional highs and lows experienced by most of her contemporaries in their pursuit of happiness.

Alice brought her up to date with what had been happening in her absence. There had been one or two minor crises, but nothing they hadn't been able to sort out, and the recent publicity in one of the glossies had brought two enquiries from people who wanted to consult Maggie as soon as she was back in England.

'Now,' said Alice, when she had finished telling their news, 'what have you been up to? Never mind the routine stuff. Get to the nitty-gritty. What did the divine Adam want?'

'He's bought a place in Spain which he wants decorated, and someone recommended us. But having discussed it with him, I don't think it's our sort of project.'

'Why ever not?' said Alice, looking amazed.

'It's in a remote part of rural Spain, a long way from Barcelona and Valencia, which is where everything we needed would have to come from. What with that dis-advantage and the Spanish *mañana* syndrome, which probably makes deliveries even more unreliable than they sometimes are here, I feel it's a job which could involve a lot of hassle.'

'But think of the prestige,' said Alice.

'I have thought—and come to the conclusion that, as Mr Rocquaine keeps his private life private, he's un-likely to allow the house to be publicised. Nor, I gather, is he planning to entertain much, so the number of people who see the place won't be large. I'm sorry, Alice. I know you would love to have been involved in designing a place for your heart-throb, but I have to look at the project from a more practical point of view. The kudos of de-signing for him wouldn't justify the headaches involved.'

'Oh, dear...what a shame,' her assistant said dis-appointedly. 'What is he like in the flesh? Where was he staying? Did you go there? How long did you spend with him?'

'He seemed pretty much the way one would expect him to be,' Maggie said non-committally. 'He was renting a house. I didn't see it. He came to Content. We talked at some length, obviously. One personal detail he let fall was that he comes from the Channel Islands. He grew up in Guernsey. Did you know that?'

Alice shook her head. 'I've never heard that before. I thought he had flats in London and New York.'

'Perhaps he has.' Maggie changed the subject by saying, 'I'd better look at my appointments book and see how soon I can fit in the other enquirers. With any luck, the places they want designed will be somewhere more accessible.'

Later that day Alice asked her again about her en-counter with Adam. Her curiosity was understandable, and in other circumstances Maggie wouldn't have minded being questioned in detail. As things were, it was difficult to speak naturally and casually of an encounter which had been an upsetting and humiliating experience for her.

'I get the impression you didn't like him much,' said Alice. 'Why not?'

Maggie shrugged. 'I prefer ordinary men to idols. Adam Rocquaine is a bit too good to be true. It's difficult to feel at ease with such a superman,' she said lightly, remembering as she spoke the night before last at Bella's Place and how easily and intimately they had talked.

'Two ordinary men are settling in downstairs. I wondered if we should ask them to lunch...as a neighbourly gesture,' said Alice.

For some weeks they had known that the second floor of the building had been leased by a video film partnership, but the new occupants hadn't moved in when Maggie left for Barbados.

'What are they like? Have you met them?' she asked.

'Only to smile and say hello on the stairs. They started setting up their equipment yesterday. They're both about thirty. One has ginger hair and freckles and the other is fair. I thought they looked nice,' said Alice.

'OK...ask them to lunch. We might as well establish friendly relations,' Maggie agreed.

That night, alone in her flat, she saw lights shining from the windows two floors below and guessed the newcomers were still busy arranging their premises. She debated taking a pot of coffee down to them in case they had no facilities for making hot drinks at present.

But her poor night's sleep on the aircraft was beginning to catch up with her, and she decided against introducing herself tonight. Probably they had almost finished whatever they were doing and would soon be going for a drink at the nearby pub or, if they were married men, hurrying home to their wives.

The next day, at lunch, she sat at the head of the table with the two men on either side of her and the rest of her staff beyond them.

The freckled man, whose light blue eyes were an uncomfortable reminder of a pair of dark blue eyes, had introduced himself as Ted Drayton, formerly a television cameraman.

His colleague and, she soon gathered, the driving force of the partnership, was William Bramshott. He had started his career as a newspaperman, turned to public relations and, for the past two years, had been the 'ideas' man behind a number of video films made for various types of businesses to use for promotional purposes.

The simple lunch, organised by Alice, began with bowls of soup followed by stir-fried vegetables and rice, cooked upstairs on Maggie's stove.

When this led William to discover that she lived at the top of the building, on her own, he said, 'Do you feel comfortable up there at night all by yourself?'

'Why not? No one can get in by the main door on the ground floor without using the entryphone, and the door of my flat has a peephole. I feel quite safe up there.'

'What about going out and coming back at night?' he asked, a rather concerned expression on his pleasant, square-cut face.

'Do I worry about being mugged, do you mean? One can't dismiss the possibility, but I don't think it's more of a risk than being knocked down by a car. I keep my eyes peeled and hope I won't be unlucky.'

'I must say this isn't an area I'd want my younger sisters to live in on their own,' said William.

Maggie asked what his sisters did and where they lived. She learned that he had three sisters and two brothers who, by the sound of it, kept in close touch with each other and were, with their parents, the sort of large, united family she had always longed to belong to.

The rice was followed by fruit and cheese. Having talked mainly to William up to that point, Maggie would have concentrated on Ted had she not seen that he and Alice seemed to be getting along particularly well.

If they hadn't all been busy people, the lunch might have gone on longer, but at five minutes to two William glanced at his watch and said they must get back to work.

'Thank you all very much. It's been fun. When we've finally got ourselves straight, you must come down and see our floor and have a drink with us,' he said, getting up from the table.

He turned to Maggie and held out his hand. 'I know women can cope with most contingencies these days, but if you're ever in need of brute strength to get something moved, or have any kind of problem which Ted and I can help with, I hope you won't hesitate to call on us.'

'Thank you, William. We'll do that.'

She gave him her hand and smiled, trying not to remember the last time a man's hand had clasped hers.

In the following fortnight Maggie threw herself into her work, allowing herself no time to think about anything else. She hoped that, if she pushed herself hard, it would have a cathartic effect and one morning she would wake up cured of the madness which had struck her in Barbados.

One evening she was working late in the studio when there was a knock on the door which startled her. Who could be calling at this hour? And how could they have got in without announcing themselves on the entryphone?

The door wasn't locked. Before she called out 'Come in,' Maggie did two things. She switched on the small cassette recorder which she often used instead of a notepad for ideas and reminders, and she took a large, sharp-bladed letter opener from its place in a pencil pot and placed it within easy reach.

'Come in.'

When William Bramshott walked in she felt foolish for taking precautions against a caller who had no right to be in the building. Engrossed in her task, she had momentarily forgotten the new tenants on the floor below.

'Still hard at it?' he said, closing the door behind him.

Maggie glanced at the clock. It was later than she had realised. 'I'm designing a wallpaper border for a collection of bedroom co-ordinates commissioned by one of the leading wallpaper and furnishing fabric companies. There are five other designers involved, all much better-known than I am, so I've got to excel myself.'

'May I see?' He came to where she was sitting and looked at the design she was colouring. 'It looks very pretty to me. I came up to ask if you'd come to the theatre with me tomorrow night? I've been offered a couple of very good seats for the new play at the Haymarket by someone who's gone down with flu. But perhaps you've already seen it?'

'No, and I'd love to go,' said Maggie, somewhat to her own surprise. 'If you like, we could have a light supper in my flat beforehand.'

'That would make a lot of extra work when you're already busy,' he objected.

'Not really, if you don't mind something basic . . . say, spaghetti bolognese and salad with a bottle of plonk.'

'Fine, but let me bring the bottle.'

After he had gone, Maggie remembered the recorder was running. She switched it off, then pressed the rewind button and played back their conversation, still faintly surprised by her immediate, eager-sounding acceptance of his invitation. Nice though he was, she wasn't in the least attracted to him. What was his motive in asking her to go out?

Perhaps, in the light of recent experience, her acceptance had been a trifle impetuous. But somehow she felt sure that William wasn't concealing a wife or a girl-friend. His straightforward character was written on his kind, open face. There was nothing devious about William.

You didn't think there was anything devious about Adam until Ella enlightened you, she reminded herself.

Adam. She could shut him out of her thoughts during the day, but she couldn't prevent him invading her dreams. Last night's dream had been particularly vivid.

How much longer is he going to haunt me? she wondered miserably.

When they came out of the theatre the following night, William insisted on seeing Maggie home.

With many other things to talk about, she had not yet found out where he lived.

'I'm sure it's miles out of your way. I'll be perfectly safe,' she assured him.

'When I take a girl out, I see her home,' he said firmly, taking hold of her elbow to steer her through the throng of departing theatregoers outside the building.

As they walked to where he had left his car in a side street, Maggie wondered how he was expecting the evening to end. She hoped it would conclude with a friendly goodnight on her doorstep, but he might have other ideas.

When she had first come to London, the so-called permissive era had still been going strong. Now things had changed, and girls who didn't want casual sex were in a stronger position to say no without being made to feel they were prudish, frigid or out of step with everyone else.

William unlocked the passenger's door for her. As he slid into the driving seat, he said, 'As a matter of fact, I live near you...in one of the gentrified streets in Spitalfields, east of Liverpool Street Station. When I bought my house it was under the threat of demolition. It's one of the Huguenot silk weavers' houses which were saved in the nick of time. Probably you've heard about them.'

'Yes—and wished I had been in a position to buy one when they were going cheap,' said Maggie. 'What I really need is a studio and showroom in the Knightsbridge-Chelsea area, but that seems an impossibility. Property prices and rents in the fashionable part of London are staggeringly high. I was lucky to get my place in Charterhouse Square. At least we have natural light and plenty of space. But it's a long way from where our customers congregate, and I think we lose business by not having a smart address.'

'You know the old saying...if a man makes a better mousetrap than his neighbour, even if he lives in the woods the world will beat a path to his door...or words to that effect,' said William. 'That's what Ted and I are counting on, anyway. Word-of-mouth recommendations are the vital thing, don't you think?'

'I hope so. Getting back to your house, aren't those weavers' houses rather large for bachelor pads? Or were you married when you bought it?'

William laughed. 'I was twenty-two and could hardly keep myself, let alone a wife. My parents helped with the mortgage, largely so that my sisters would have somewhere to live when they wanted to come and work in London, as the provincial young invariably do. Now two of them are married and the youngest is living at home in Bath to be near the guy she's got her eye on. I'm the only one who's still unattached. How about you? Have you been married...or attached?'

'Too busy making my way in the world,' said Maggie. 'I notice you spoke of hardly being able to keep yourself, let alone a wife. Do you think of a wife as being a dependant rather than someone to share the overheads?'

He took a few moments to answer. 'I suppose I do, yes. Not immediately perhaps, but eventually. Comes of having a mother who's never worked outside the home, I guess. My parents started a family straight away and, as my father's a doctor, my mother has always been involved in his work...answering the telephone and so on.'

For a time after arriving at the square they sat in the car, exchanging extracts from their life stories. Earlier, over supper, they had kept to impersonal topics.

At length Maggie said, 'Thank you very much for taking me to the play, William. It's ages since I've been to the theatre and I thoroughly enjoyed it.'

'I enjoyed your cooking. It's been a good evening, hasn't it? We must do it again.'

'Yes ... I'd like to. Please don't bother to get out. It's starting to drizzle. There's no point in your getting damp.'

'Sit tight a minute.' As she made to get out, he put a restraining hand on her arm and stretched his other arm round the back of his seat to produce an umbrella.

A few minutes later he was holding it over her while she unlocked the door.

'Look, this isn't a line, I promise you, but shall I see you as far as your own door?' he suggested.

'It's kind of you, William, but it really isn't necessary. I've never been afraid of the dark,' she assured him, not quite truthfully.

It wasn't that she suspected him of being motivated by anything but chivalry. It was merely that she knew her underlying dislike of the gloomy staircase at night could easily get out of hand if she let it.

'OK ... if you're sure,' he said doubtfully. 'See you tomorrow, I expect.'

'I expect so. Goodnight.' From inside the hallway she smiled at him.

'Goodnight.' He touched his fingers to his lips and blew her a kiss before walking away.

The gesture took Maggie's mind off the rather creepy atmosphere of the stairs at night and the sound of her footsteps mounting the bare stone treads. She could imagine him bidding a similar farewell to his mother and sisters, or to friends of his sisters whom he had known since they were children.

The kiss he had blown to her seemed to put their relationship on the same comfortable footing. William wasn't the sort of man who would sweep a girl off her feet within hours of meeting her, she thought approvingly. No doubt he had sown some wild oats when he was younger, but she felt sure that now, if he made love to a woman, it would not be from careless impulse but because he genuinely cared for her.

The following Monday morning he returned from a weekend in the country with sprays of wintersweet from his mother's garden, which he brought up to the studio when Maggie was having her coffee-break.

'Next Sunday I'm giving a brunch party. I'd like you to come, if you're free,' he said.

Maggie accepted the invitation. For the rest of the week the yellow flowers on the otherwise bare branches filled her office with their delicate fragrance and a promise of spring.

On Sunday morning she dressed in silver-grey needlecord jeans and a violet silk shirt under a blackberry-dark sweater which she could take off if William's house was warm. He had sketched a map to help her find it.

His early-eighteenth-century front door was opened not by William himself but by a schoolboy whose twin sister took charge of Maggie's mac and directed her to go upstairs to the first floor drawing-room.

The walls of the hall and staircase had their original pine panelling, painted a soft bluey-green, and the uncarpeted stairs showed the wear of many generations of feet passing up and down them. Like all old houses, this one gave Maggie a sense of stability and continuity, and she envied William his possession of it.

The sound of voices and laughter led her to a large room where a log fire was burning and about a dozen people were already occupying the window-seats and some shabby but comfortable-looking sofas and chairs.

Not everyone was talking. Several were reading the Sunday papers, of which there was a stack by the door.

On the other side of the doorway was a table on which two bottles of champagne stood in a plastic bucket of ice flanked by cartons of orange juice and a collection of tall glasses, goblets, mugs and tankards.

'Hello. Which would you like? Champagne...orange juice...or Buck's?' asked the man in charge of this array.

'Orange juice, please.'

As she waited for him to pour it, William appeared and put his arm lightly round her shoulders. 'Hi! You made it. Come and be introduced. Not everyone here is fully awake yet, so we'll leave them to surface gradually. What—no bubbly? Come on, a dash won't hurt, even if you haven't eaten yet.'

Being uncertain what time the brunch would materialise, she had taken the precaution of having a boiled egg and toast before setting out. With champagne added to her orange juice, she was introduced to a group which included an Indian girl in a rose-red sari, an *au pair* from West Germany and a tall, bearded Canadian.

Maggie had never had difficulty getting on with strangers, and William's guests were an interesting mixture of nationalities, ages and backgrounds. They continued to arrive for some time, the party overflowing from the drawing-room until the whole house seemed to be full of people.

The food—everyone helping themselves from a spread in the kitchen—was simple and plentiful. Cold meats and various smoked fish. Baked potatoes. Garlic bread. Salad. Pickles. French and English cheeses. Interesting biscuits.

Maggie ate her brunch sitting on a cushion on the stairs with a man who made his living painting murals and his girlfriend who made up models for photographic assignments. William was busy going round with a bottle of white wine in one hand and red in the other, replenishing his guests' glasses.

'Have you eaten anything yet?' Maggie asked, when he came to them.

'Don't worry about me. I've been snacking all morning. There are plenty more baked potatoes if you could manage another, David.' He smiled and moved on, a genial host who obviously enjoyed entertaining and had a gift for making friends.

'Nice bloke, old William,' said the muralist. 'Give you the shirt off his back if he thought you needed it.'

Later on Maggie had taken her plate back to the basement where the teenage twins were now washing dishes in a modernised scullery, and was helping herself to fruit salad from an enormous transfer-printed blue and white footbath, when someone said, 'Are you Maggie Hornchurch?'

She turned to find a woman with dark brown hair and strikingly beautiful topaz eyes smiling at her.

'I'm Laurian Thornham. William was going to introduce us, but he's been too busy. I'm also a designer, but my field is clothes.'

'I know. I have one of your suits.'

Although she didn't want to be reminded of the last time she had heard of Laurian and her husband Oliver, Maggie couldn't help taking an instant liking to her.

'I wonder if the fruit salad has lashings of kirsch in it? As you can see, I'm pregnant, so I've sworn off alc. for the duration,' said Laurian.

Maggie tasted a spoonful of the liquid from her bowl. 'It doesn't taste strongly alcoholic.'

'In that case, I'll have some.' As she dipped the ladle into the fruit, Laurian went on, 'We live just a few doors from here. When William came to pot-luck supper the other night, he told us that you inhabit the two floors above his new studio. I was particularly interested because I'd been planning to contact you after seeing some of your work in the last issue of *House & Garden*. My husband and I are looking for someone to design the interiors of two houses in Spain. They're in a ghost town which Oliver is bringing back to life. Does the idea interest you?'

'Does one of the houses belong to Adam Rocquaine?'

Laurian gave her a surprised glance. 'No...but he does have a house there. Has he approached you about it?'

'We met in Barbados recently. He did ask me if I would do it, but I turned it down.'

Laurian looked even more surprised. 'Why was that? Are you too busy?'

'I am busy, yes. But I also took into account the problems of working in a remote part of Spain.'

The other girl smiled. 'Millions of women would consider that any problems involved would be far outweighed by the pleasure of working for Adam. He is rather gorgeous, don't you think?'

Before Maggie could reply, a very tall, dark-haired man slipped his arm round Laurian's waist and said, 'Are you talking about me?'

She laughed. 'No—but you're in the same league. Maggie...this is my husband. This is Maggie Hornchurch, the interior designer, darling. I've just started to tell her about Pobla de Cabres.'

'How do you do, Miss Hornchurch. My wife tells me you're an extremely talented designer. Can we interest you in an involvement in one of the most exciting projects going on in Europe?' he asked, as they shook hands.

Maggie could see that it wasn't only wifely bias which made Laurian put him in the same league as Adam.

'Having turned Mr Rocquaine down, wouldn't it be rather unethical for me to take on other houses there?' she suggested.

Oliver Thornham raised his eyebrows. 'You turned down his house? Why?'

Maggie repeated the explanation she had given to Laurian.

He gave her a thoughtful look before he said, 'Let me congratulate you on your admirable common sense, Miss Hornchurch. As I overheard my wife say to you, the majority of your sex would have ignored any difficulties if it gave them a chance to associate with Adam Rocquaine, or rather the image of Rocquaine projected by his promoters. In my view, the real man is rather different from his public persona. You, very sensibly, haven't allowed that to influence you. If your taste is as sound as your judgement, you are definitely the person we want for the houses Laurian has told you about. Let's find a quiet corner where we can tell you more about them.'

There was something about Oliver Thornham which made Maggie feel that his good opinion wasn't easily won by members of his own sex and even more rarely by the opposite sex. She could imagine his disdain if he knew how easily she had succumbed to Adam's charm in Barbados. She longed to know exactly what he had meant by saying that in his opinion the real Adam was different from the image the public had of him. But, if he didn't like Adam, why had he allowed him to buy into Pobla de Cabres?

'I think all the quiet corners are already occupied,' said Laurian. 'Would you like some fruit salad, darling?'

Her husband shook his head. 'We'll find somewhere,' he said confidently.

Five minutes later, with William's permission, they were ensconced in what had once been the silk weaver's garret at the top of the house and was now his bedroom.

'You are absolutely right in concluding there would be problems if you agreed to work with us at Pobla de Cabres,' said Oliver, when they were comfortably settled. 'I had to overcome numerous difficulties before I was given permission, at government level, to redevelop the village before it degenerated into a huddle of ruins. Even my architect, who belongs to one of Catalonia's most influential families, has had problems. If the building of one holiday villa in Spain is not without snags, it follows that the restoration of an entire village is riddled with difficulties and setbacks. I won't delude you on that score.'

'I should think you'll put her off entirely,' murmured Laurian, with an amused but loving look at her husband's rather stern face. She turned to Maggie. 'Oliver is right, of course, but on the other hand Pobla de Cabres is the most lovely place. If you saw it, I don't think you'd be able to resist it. I've a good idea: when the party breaks up, come and have tea at our place and we'll show you some photographs of the village and the two houses whose owners have deputed us to organise the interior décor for them.'

'An excellent suggestion,' said Oliver. 'I expect you're wondering why people should have bought the shells of houses at Pobla de Cabres if they haven't the time or interest to supervise making them habitable.'

'Yes, I am,' Maggie agreed. 'And also whether my work is likely to please them. Far from preferring *carte blanche*, most interior designers dislike working without a brief. The whole object of the exercise is to create an appropriate setting for the client, not a showcase for the designer's pet ideas.'

Oliver nodded. 'So I gather.' He began to explain why the owners of these particular houses wanted most of the decisions to be taken for them.

During the following week Maggie spent every spare moment trying to come to a decision about Pobla de Cabres.

Her visit to the Thornhams' house for tea and hot buttered crumpets had confirmed her liking for them both; and the photographs they had shown her had more than supported Laurian's claim that the deserted village in a valley surrounded by mountains in a part of Spain known to few tourists was an idyllic place.

Had she never met Adam, Maggie would have jumped at the chance to design the two interiors. It was the risk of another encounter with him which made her hesitate to accept.

Oliver—a man of swift decisions himself—had given her a week to make up her mind. But on Wednesday morning Laurian rang up to say she was giving a dinner party on Saturday night and hoped Maggie and William could come, if they were free at such short notice.

'I am. I don't know about William,' said Maggie, wondering if Laurian imagined they were more involved with each other than was in fact the case.

'If you are, I'm sure he will be.'

What did that mean? Maggie wondered. Aloud she said, 'What time?'

'Seven-thirty for eight.'

'Black tie?' asked Maggie, to get some idea of what she should wear. Dinner party was an elastic term which could stretch from a kitchen table by candlelight to something far more elaborate.

'No, no—nothing formal,' said Laurian. 'I shall be wearing trousers and a glittery sweater, if that helps. By the way, I did enjoy our gossip by the fire on Sunday. I hope we'll get time for some more shop-talk on Sunday.'

Maggie hoped so, too. She had the feeling that she and Laurian could become really close friends. But did the other woman like her well enough to keep in touch if Maggie turned down Pobla de Cabres?

Later in the day William telephoned to tell her he was also going to the Thornhams' party and to offer to take her there and run her home in his car.

'It's very kind of you, but I can easily get a taxi.'

'I wouldn't hear of it. I'll be there about seven-twenty.'

At twenty-nine minutes past seven on Saturday night, Maggie sat by the entryphone receiver in her flat, wondering what had happened to delay him.

She had been ready and waiting to run down the stairs since seven-fifteen. If he didn't turn up soon, they would be late arriving, which wouldn't bother some people but did worry Maggie. Punctuality was important to her—and also, she felt sure, to Oliver Thornham. There would have to be a very good reason for him to take a lenient view of guests who failed to turn up in good time for a meal at his table.

At that moment the entryphone buzzed.

'William?'

'Yes. Sorry I'm late. I'll explain when you come down.'

It turned out he had been driving behind a car which had been hit by another car. He had felt duty-bound to stop and offer himself as a witness of the accident. It had taken longer than he had anticipated.

As it was almost eight when he rang the Thornhams' bell, it wasn't surprising to find they were the last-comers.

About a dozen people were drinking sherry and chatting in the elegant first-floor drawing-room which Maggie guessed had been designed by Laurian because at a rapid glance it showed a sure and highly individual taste but none of the distinguishing marks of the leading professionals.

As William knew the house, it hadn't been necessary for the housekeeper who had admitted them to bring them upstairs. As soon as they entered the softly lit, flower-filled room, their hostess came to welcome and introduce them.

William seemed to have met most of the other guests. To Maggie they were all strangers; or so she thought until, with shock and dismay, she found herself face to face with Adam Rocquaine.

'Adam you've already met,' Laurian was saying, as Maggie recoiled from the sight of him.

If he had been equally surprised to see her coming into the room, he had had time to mask his reaction. 'Yes, quite recently,' he said, taking the hand she had offered automatically, but not retaining his hold on it as he had on the beach in Barbados. Nor did he smile.

When the introductions had been completed, Oliver gave Maggie a glass of sherry and stayed talking to her and the last person to whom she and William had been introduced until it was time for them all to go down to the ground-floor dining-room.

To Maggie's relief, Adam was seated on the same side of the table as herself, but with several people between them. The meal wasn't ruined for her by having to make polite conversation to him. She couldn't even see him. But merely knowing he was there was disturbing. She wondered what would happen after the meal: whether he would talk to her or ignore her.

'That, as you probably realise, is a portrait of my wife as a child,' said Oliver Thornham.

Everyone had returned to the drawing-room, and Maggie had been studying a painting of Laurian sitting by the sea, looking like a mermaid.

As she turned to look at her host who was holding a tray with several cups of black coffee and a cream jug and sugar bowl on it, he said, 'Have you come to a decision?'

A few hours earlier she had intended to say yes, she would take on the houses at Pobla de Cabres. Now the upsetting effect of meeting Adam again had raised fresh doubts in her mind.

Before she could answer Oliver's question, they were joined by Adam himself.

He said to his host, 'Have you succeeded where I failed? Have you persuaded Maggie to come in on the Spanish project?'

'I don't know yet. She's about to tell me that. Coffee?' Oliver offered him the tray.

Maggie found that her mental processes were affected by Adam's nearness in the same way that steel affected the function of a compass.

She watched his strong, sunburned hand take a fragile porcelain demitasse from the antique lacquer tray, aware of a hemmed-in sensation with the two powerfully built men towering over her, even though she was wearing her highest heels.

Rather surprisingly, it was the entrepreneur, not the singing star, who was dressed with panache. Oliver was wearing a black velvet smoking jacket with a pale grey shirt and a pink scarf knotted inside the open collar.

It was Adam who was conservatively turned out in a dark blue pinstripe suit with a waistcoat and a discreet shirt and tie. A dark red silk handkerchief loosely tucked into his breast pocket was the only flamboyant note, and not one which would have raised any eyebrows in the most reactionary men's club. Indeed, tonight his appearance was the acme of English conservatism. Any foreigner seeing him might have supposed that he spent his days in one of the stuffier merchant banks or perhaps in command of a troop of Horse Guards, the immaculate sheen on his black shoes being the achievement of his batman.

'I detect indecision...to which my presence tonight may have contributed. Am I right, Maggie?' he asked.

As, reluctantly, she lifted her gaze to meet his, he continued, 'Let me talk to her, will you, Oliver? I have something to say which may persuade her to say yes.'

CHAPTER THREE

WHEN Oliver had moved away, Adam turned to look at the painting of Laurian Thornham.

'One can see why the artist called this portrait *Neptune's Daughter*. It was on the West Indian island where Laurian grew up that I first met the Thornhams. They're a remarkable couple... very well-matched. I'll be surprised if they aren't still together in twenty or thirty years' time.' His deep blue gaze switched from the picture to Maggie. 'The man you arrived with... what is his connection with you?'

The question surprised and disconcerted her. She was tempted to answer that it was not his business. After a pause she said stiffly, 'William makes video films in the building where I have my studio. He's my neighbour during the day and a near neighbour of the Thornhams at night. He has the luck to own one of these beautiful houses.'

'Oh, you met on arrival, did you? I thought he had brought you to the party.'

'He did... and he's taking me home,' she added, on a self-protective impulse.

'I see. Were you involved with him when you came to Barbados?'

'Did you cross-examine your neighbours at dinner like this? Has it suddenly become the thing to ask personal questions?' she asked him, raising her eyebrows.

'You and I are not strangers, Maggie,' he answered drily.

The memory of his lips on her mouth pierced her with strange sensations, mingling pleasure with pain.

'You had something to say to me,' she reminded him.

'Yes.' Adam drained the small cup and replaced it on its gold-rimmed saucer, putting them down on the table beneath the portrait, a painted console bearing an arrangement of dried flowers and grasses in a basket made of lavender stalks.

He said, 'Whether or not you were involved with Bramshott at the time we met, I was not—as you found out—alone in Barbados. That association is over. There is now no "just impediment" why we shouldn't be friends—if you will take my word that I didn't deceive you deliberately.'

He sounded sincerely contrite. In an instant all the emotions which had burgeoned during their evening together at Bella's Place revived and filled her with longing to believe him.

Determined to keep her head, she said guardedly, 'But how can any deception ever be anything but deliberate?'

'We were only together for a short time. Believe me, I would have taken you into my confidence if we'd spent a second evening together. Don't let what happened put you off taking this assignment with the Thornhams. You don't have to do my house as well if you don't want to. But I think you'll be missing an important and enjoyable opportunity if you turn them down.'

'Hear, hear,' said Laurian, joining them in time to hear this last remark. 'But you aren't going to turn us down, are you, Maggie?'

There was a pause during which they both looked at her expectantly, Laurian with smiling confidence, Adam looking less certain.

Maggie found herself saying, 'I think I should be considered a bit off my rocker if I did. Yes, I'll tackle your two houses, Laurian, but whether I can cope with three, I'm not sure. I think I had better reserve judgement on that.'

'Splendid! That's settled, then,' said the other girl, looking pleased. 'Now come and meet Arabella Gunton, who is longing to talk to you but didn't like to butt in while you were being monopolised by the man whose latest title is Mr Irresistible.'

This piece of banter did not amuse Adam. In fact, he looked quite annoyed.

'Where did you read that rubbish? In one of the tabloids, I suppose?'

'Yes, in my daily's favourite rag. Don't you look at your press cuttings?'

'Not if I can avoid it. Inaccurate piffle, most of them,' he said dismissively.

Laurian laughed and led Maggie away. When next she glanced in Adam's direction he was in conversation with two other men, the gravity of their expressions suggesting the topic was a serious one.

Although she was trying to concentrate on her own conversation with Mrs Gunton, her mind kept flitting away to examine what Adam had said to her. She wondered why he had dispensed with the blonde—for it seemed unlikely that she would have ended the relationship.

Presently William joined them and, when Mrs Gunton had moved away, said quietly to Maggie, 'I haven't had a chance to tell you how nice you look. Well, you always look nice, but particularly stunning tonight in that unusual skirt.'

'Thank you. I'm glad you like it.'

She glanced down at her full skirt. She had had it made up from an old Paisley shawl whose colours time had mellowed to subtle coppery reds and browns which echoed the auburn lights in her thick hair. With it she was wearing a very plain cream silk blouse, with a pretty Victorian brooch pinned to a length of antique silk-velvet ribbon which she had made into a choker.

'I don't know much about women's clothes,' he went on, 'but somehow yours always make other people's look ordinary.'

She smiled at him. 'Thank you again—but you can't say Laurian looks ordinary. The colours in that sweater she's wearing are wonderful.'

'Yes, but clothes are her thing. I don't much care for that pink outfit,' he confided in an undertone, his eyes on the only badly dressed woman in the room.

It wasn't until he was driving her back to Charterhouse Square that he said, 'What did you think of Adam Rocquaine? I noticed him chatting you up. I thought he seemed rather nicer than one would expect. Not too full of himself or inclined to hold the floor at dinner.'

'No, he seemed very pleasant,' she agreed.

William glanced sideways at her. 'That's rather a tepid reaction to one of God's gifts to women, isn't it?'

'The only man in the limelight whom I admire is Prince Charles,' she answered evasively. 'He really is my *beau idéal*.'

'Don't you like Rocquaine's music? Most women seem to.'

'I prefer it to a lot of pop—yes. But I don't rush out to buy his new records the way Alice does.'

To deflect his thoughts from Adam, she remarked on the excellent food the Thornhams had given them.

'My parents always say that the best part of a party is discussing it afterwards,' William remarked, as he turned the car into the narrow street which led to her corner of the square.

The trees were leafless at the moment, but in summer they cast a pleasant shade over the little park where workers from the surrounding buildings could sit on the grass in their lunch-breaks.

Very near Smithfield Market, the scene for seven hundred years of Bartholomew Fair, England's most famous cloth fair, and St Bartholomew's Hospital, popularly known as Bart's, with a medical school where thousands of doctors had trained, the square was in one of the most historic parts of London. But not many tourists discovered it and, at this hour of night, there was no hint of the Hogarthian bustle which went on in the market between five and nine in the morning.

Tonight there was no need for William to reach behind him for the umbrella before jumping out to come round and open the nearside door for her.

'There's a concert at the Barbican Arts Centre next week which I'd like to go to—if you'll come with me,' he said. 'Are you free next Thursday?'

'Yes, but I think I should warn you my musical taste is definitely middle-brow.'

'Mine, too. I'll show you the programme on Monday. If you don't fancy it, we could go to the theatre again.'

'All right . . . but let's make it a Dutch treat.'

Instead of agreeing, he said, 'Why?'

'Everything is so expensive, William. Why should it all fall on you? Most people do go Dutch now, especially if the girl has a good job.'

'And suspects the man might expect a return on his investment which she doesn't want to give,' he said sardonically. 'But I don't happen to be that type, Maggie.'

'I never thought you were,' she assured him. 'But as I'm sure you've often split the bill after a night out with one of your men friends, and I often have with my women friends, why shouldn't friends of different sexes do the same?'

'I'll tell you... but not right now. It's late, and in a moment of madness I promised to spend tomorrow helping friends to move house. Only from south of the river to north of the park, but they're expecting me there bright and early.'

As she took her keys from her bag, he removed them from her hand and unlocked the outer door for her.

'Thank you for driving me there and back,' she said, as he returned them to her.

'My pleasure. Goodnight.' He put both hands lightly on her shoulder and kissed her, first on one cheek and then on the other.

For a moment she thought there was going to be a third kiss—on her lips. But evidently William decided that, like his explanation of why they shouldn't go Dutch, it must wait.

Maggie spent Sunday morning at her drawing-board. On fine spring and summer Sundays she would catch a bus to the parks or to the Embankment to walk by the river. By this stage of the winter she was beginning to long for the first daffodils from the Scillies to herald another spring.

As soon as she stopped concentrating on the problem of what to do with a cramped and badly lit hall in a house in Kensington, and started preparing her lunch, thoughts of Adam and William crowded into her mind.

She felt in her bones that William could become serious about her, and she about him—if she had never met Adam.

William had all the qualities she liked in a man: kindness, a sense of humour, enthusiasm for his work, but not the aggressive drive to make money which had characterised her first stepfather, whose principal attraction for her mother had been the way he lavished it on her. Excellence rather than riches was what Maggie felt a man, or a woman, should strive for. In that and other respects, she felt she and William were two of a kind.

But the touch of his lips on her cheeks had not had the same effect as Adam's first handshake.

Thinking of Adam, she wondered why he had made a point of telling her that his liaison with the blonde was over, but then allowed Laurian to whisk her away to meet someone else and not spoken to her again, not even to say goodnight.

He had left the party early, slipping out of the room so discreetly that probably Maggie was the only person—other than his hosts—who had noticed him leave. Later she had heard Laurian say that today he was flying to Sydney to appear in a special all-star charity show at the Opera House.

Would he contact her when he came back? 'You and I are not strangers, Maggie.' Had he said that only to remind her how quickly she had succumbed to his magnetism? Or could it possibly be that he, too, had felt . . . No, no, it couldn't, she told herself firmly.

The next day, driven by an irresistible compulsion, she bought his most recent album—*Do You Remember Babylon?*

On the sleeve was a picture of Adam's strong profile silhouetted against a flaming sunset with a shadowy impression of an Eastern garden in the background.

The album took its title from the first song on side one which, the sleeve notes explained, had been inspired by lines from a Victorian poem—'When I was a king in Babylon and you were a Christian slave.'

That evening Maggie played it again and again till she knew both the tune and the words by heart. The lyric was about a man who had been parted from a girl in Babylon, centuries ago, and was still searching the world for her.

Maggie's intelligence told her that it was an idea calculated to appeal to vast numbers of the female sex who had yet to meet the man of their dreams. At the same time her heart persuaded her that only a man who believed in love, and was searching for it, could have written such a song.

Do you remember the fountains...the scent of roses...the moonlight?

Later, lying in the bath, most of her body still browner than the places which had been covered by her bikini, she found herself humming the melody and thinking, again, about the man who had composed it and who would by now be asleep on his flight to Australia.

But, even if he were awake, it was highly improbable he would be thinking of her. She doubted if he had given her a thought since leaving the party.

Maggie's first visit to Spain took place three weeks later, by which time she had been out with William several times but had heard nothing from Adam. For all she knew, he might still be on the other side of the world.

Her flight to Barcelona was an early one. There she was met by Diego Montfalcó, Oliver's architect, and his English wife, Lucinda. They had been spending the weekend with his parents, who lived in Spain's second largest city.

In a fast car, using the motorway, the rest of the journey didn't take long. Much of the way, the Mediterranean was in view, and they stopped for lunch at a small town on the coast. Afterwards they turned inland and a little more than half an hour later Lucinda was able to point out Pobla de Cabres in the distance.

She and her husband were the first of the village's new residents, and had offered to put Maggie up. They had a little girl, Rosa, but she was staying with her grandparents until Lucinda drove Maggie back to the airport and collected the child.

As soon as Maggie had unpacked her case, Lucinda took her on a tour of the village. As the population at its largest had been fewer than five hundred people, housed in large family groups of several generations, it didn't take long to walk from one end to the other.

'This is the Abercorns' house,' said Lucinda, taking her into a building on the outskirts of the village. 'I expect Laurian has told you that Mrs Abercorn suffers from emphysema and needs a mild winter climate. Her husband has been working in the Middle East with the object of retiring early and bringing her to Spain. I'm not sure they wouldn't have done better to go to the extreme south, weather-wise, but they want a quiet life, not the glitz of Marbella.'

The other house Maggie had to look at was in the centre of the *pueblo*, with no views except from a small flat roof used by its previous owners for hanging out washing.

'The Bedales are sailing people. They've spent thirty years living on board a ketch, but now they're on their last voyage. They haven't even seen the place yet,' said Lucinda. 'They bought it unseen because they know and trust Oliver. He says Fanny Bedale is almost indistinguishable from her husband. Her favourite garment is a fisherman's slop and she has a complexion like treebark. She could sail the Atlantic single-handed if she had to, but she wouldn't know where to begin doing up a house.'

'Where is Adam Rocquaine's house?' asked Maggie, as they left the Bedales' place.

'I'll show you. Are you doing his as well?'

'He asked me to, but at the time I didn't think I could fit it in with my other work. However, with two other houses to do here I might be able to manage it.'

'His house is not far from the pool,' said Lucinda. 'I haven't shown you that yet. It's my husband's *pièce de résistance*, or will be when it's completed. He can't stand Hollywood-style pools which look like flakes of Day-Glo blue paint when you see them from the air. The pool here is going to be landscaped to look as natural as possible, although as there will be a lot of American owners there will have to be a jacuzzi in the pool area.'

Although interested in the pool layout, Maggie was even more interested in seeing the house Adam had described to her in Barbados.

The knocker on the massive front door was a woman's hand and embroidered cuff, cast in brass which was now badly tarnished.

'You see those on many Spanish houses, but that one is larger than most,' said Lucinda, when Maggie remarked on it.

Only twice in her career had she worked on houses in which, the first time she saw them, she had felt a special sense of excitement, knowing almost at once what was needed to enhance their best features.

It happened for the third time in Adam's house. As she went from room to room the character of the house impressed her as strongly as, on the beach outside Content, she had felt its owner's charisma.

'I think this one has far more possibilities than the other two, but of course, being three houses in one, it's much larger than they are,' said Lucinda.

Presently, over tea in her house, she told Maggie how she and her husband had met while she was living in a *casita* among the rice fields round the mouth of the Ebro river.

Later Diego joined them, and he and Maggie talked while Lucinda prepared the evening meal.

'I can hear a car coming,' she told them, some time later when she came back to the simply furnished living-room with a tray of *tapas*—pickled anchovies, cubes of Manchego cheese and several different types of olives. 'I wonder who's coming to see us?'

'I'm not expecting any visitors tonight,' said Diego.

A few minutes later they heard a car in first gear coming up the steep narrow street which led to the grandly named Plaza Mayor, the square in front of the church which was the only place to park a vehicle at the top of the village.

'I'll go and see who it is. Excuse me.'

Diego disappeared, leaving Maggie to rise from her chair and cross the room to a large bookcase. She was looking through the illustrations in a book on Antonio Gaudí, the most famous of all Spanish architects, when she heard Diego returning and calling out, 'Can we feed another mouth, Lucinda?'

'Of course... who is it?' As she asked, his wife must have looked out of the doorway to the kitchen. An instant later, she said, 'Oh, hello... what brings you here?'

Then a voice which made Maggie's heart lurch said, 'I had a couple of free days, so I thought I'd fly down and see how things are going.' Then, in Spanish, *'Como estas, señora?'* to which Lucinda rattled off a reply in her husband's language, making Maggie think that perhaps the other man's voice had only sounded like Adam's.

But it was Adam who, moments later, strolled into the living-room. And he didn't seem at all surprised to see her, making her wonder if he had known she was here.

'You two have met before, I believe?' said Diego.

'Yes, indeed. How are you, Maggie?' Adam came to shake hands.

'Very well, thanks. And you?' Each time they met she was startled afresh by the intense blue of his eyes.

'Fine... but looking forward to a few days' peace and quiet.'

'How was your trip to Australia?' she asked.

'The concert was a sell-out. I think the rock stars had more to do with that than I had, but between us we raised a lot of money for a good cause. After that I went to Japan and then to Vancouver. I don't seem to have touched down anywhere for more than forty-eight hours since I last saw you,' he told her, with a wry smile.

'In that case, I'm surprised you came here instead of to your house in Guernsey.' She didn't want to sound pleased to see him. She wasn't sure that she was.

'The weather forecast for the Channel Islands is rain. I wanted some sun to relax in.'

Lucinda joined them. 'If we'd known you were flying in today, we could have shown Maggie a few of the sights of Barcelona and all driven down together... saved you renting a car.'

'I didn't feel like driving down, so I came by Apache, with a car laid on at the airfield for me,' he explained casually.

'Flying yourself, or with a pilot?' asked Diego.

'Flying myself. Half an hour in the air is a lot less tiring than two hours plus on the *autopista*. Are you sure your evening meal will stretch to include me?' he asked Lucinda.

'Easily,' she assured him. 'We can offer you a bed, too... unless you prefer to stay at the hotel in San Carlos?'

'I have a reservation there... but I'd much rather stay here if it won't put you out.'

'Not a bit. I showed Maggie your house this afternoon.'

'What did you think of it, Maggie?' Adam asked, turning to her.

'I thought the conversion had been extremely well thought out,' she answered, including Diego in her reply. 'It needs the kind of interior John Stefanidis has done for Greek island houses. He would probably do it for you if you approached him.'

'There's only one designer I want to do it,' said Adam. 'But I won't press you on that subject tonight. Before I sample those olives, Lucinda, may I wash my hands?'

She led him away. When they had left the room, Diego said, 'Why did you recommend Stefanidis to him? He's a fine designer and I agree that his style is suited to the houses here, although possibly a little more spartan than some of the owners would like. But don't you want to design the interior yourself?'

She couldn't tell him the real reason why she had doubts about working for Adam. She said, 'Very much, but I seem to be the only designer Adam knows about, and I like to feel my clients have chosen me for sound reasons, not because they were unaware of their options.'

'I don't think you need to worry about taking advantage of Adam,' the Spaniard remarked, with a slight smile. 'He has the reputation of being extremely astute. Oliver was impressed by his grasp of financial matters. Don't let the fact that he rented an aeroplane to get here from Barcelona mislead you. In show-business terms, he isn't an extravagant man.'

When Adam reappeared he had changed his shirt, making Maggie wish she had put on something different for the evening. She was still in the clothes she had set out in, a cream silk shirt with beige gabardine trousers and a plaited leather belt. To which, when dressing that morning, she had added a fine wool blazer in brown and beige checks and a camel-coloured cashmere muffler. It was the American designer Ralph Lauren's style, achieved for a lot less money than the authentic look by careful shopping around for clothes in the Lauren manner at budget prices.

Lucinda's chicken in almond sauce not only stretched to four, but allowed the two men to have second helpings. Supper, served at a pine table with rush mats on it, was a cheerful meal with a second bottle of wine from the vineyards of Miguel Torres, the Catalan winemaker of increasing renown, following the first.

Although the day had been warm and sunny, as darkness had fallen over the surrounding mountains the temperature had dropped. While they were eating, Diego put a match to the fire laid on the stone hearth. Soon a large log from an olive tree was burning, adding firelight to the soft effulgence of the candles on the table.

'Next month Lucinda has to go to London to promote a book partly written by her grandfather and partly by her,' said Diego. 'She's dreading it, aren't you, sweetie? Is there any advice you can give her, Adam? I suppose you're so used to the limelight, you've forgotten any nervousness you may have felt in your early days as a performer.'

'Some experienced performers continue to suffer from stage-fright throughout their careers,' Adam answered. 'I don't myself, and I doubt if Lucinda will when it comes to the point.' He smiled at her. 'Just be your natural self and you can't go wrong.'

'Easier said than done, I fancy. Have you ever been on TV or radio, Maggie?' Lucinda asked.

'No, but I'd like the chance to air my views,' said Maggie. 'For instance, I think it's such a shame that schoolchildren aren't taught to discriminate between good and bad architecture, good and bad furniture and so on. I'd love to hold forth on that pet subject. Judging by what you were telling me this afternoon, Lucinda, your grandfather was a fascinating man. I shouldn't think listeners and viewers could fail to be interested in him.'

'The trick is to forget about the listeners and viewers and pretend you're having a private chat with the interviewer,' said Adam. 'No matter how large my audience is, I sing my songs to one person.'

'A real person?' Lucinda asked him.

'Yes.'

'How intriguing. May we know who she is?'

'My grandmother... who is dead now. But if I'm appearing on TV I still look through the lens of the camera and see her in her favourite chair, stitching away at her needlepoint while I play for her.'

'How old were you when you started composing songs?' asked Diego.

'About fifteen or sixteen. I'm not a good pianist, but I was able to pick out a tune on the piano as quite a small boy and my grandmother played well enough to teach me as much as I needed to know. If it had involved taking proper piano lessons, I would have opted out. Teenage boys of my generation had to be seriously musical to put up with the ribbing they got from the ones who were into sport and sailing. I had a pretty macho image of myself at sixteen. Writing songs about unrequited love was a strictly *sub rosa* exercise.'

'Why songs about unrequited love? I can't believe you were ever the sort of boy girls ignore,' said Lucinda.

'I wasn't interested in girls of my own age. I was in love with an older woman. She must have been about the same age you are now, Lucinda. She lived in the house next door. I used to watch her gardening from my bedroom window. On days when it rained and she didn't appear, I wrote poems to her,' he added with a grin, before asking Diego how he had come to choose architecture as a career.

After supper they sat round the fire, Lucinda and her husband sharing a sofa and their guests in armchairs. The conversation ranged over many subjects and Maggie discovered that, like Diego, Adam spoke several languages.

When Lucinda remarked that it was unusual to come across a polyglot Englishman, he said, with his characteristic shrug, 'I spend a lot of my life in transit. I try to use the time constructively. Probably one of the reasons why my records do well in Spain is because I speak enough Spanish to appear on their chat shows.'

It was late when they went to bed, Maggie in a room with a view of the moonlit sierras which, unlike the much higher peaks of the Pyrenees over which she had flown that morning, had no snow on their crests. Here, so Lucinda had told her, there was seldom snow on the mountains, and the almond trees had blossomed some weeks earlier.

She was woken by the fiery glow of sunrise. Knowing that in the next hour or two the landscape would be at its best, she got up and washed and dressed, putting on knee-length shorts and a warm sweater over her shirt.

Creeping stealthily down the stairs in order not to disturb the others, she found the main door unlocked and let herself out. She had with her a camera and a sketch-pad.

As the sky became streaked with colour and the light of morning spread a roseate glaze over the coral clay tiles of the ancient roofs, she used a whole roll of film on the *plaza* and the narrow streets leading off it.

She was sketching one of the projecting wooden balconies which were a feature of the village when Adam's voice made her jump.

'Good morning. Would you like to share my apple?'

Before she had collected her wits, he had cut the apple in two with a Swiss army knife and was offering half of it to her.

'Good morning... thank you.' Maggie put down her pen and accepted it.

She was sitting on a lightweight camp stool which she always packed in the bottom of her case as part of her sketching equipment. 'You're up early.'

'That's what my body-clock tells me,' Adam said drily. 'It's still on Canadian time.' He gave a smiling shrug. 'Like long-haul air crew, I spend a lot of my life in a state of jet lag. As with any chronic condition, one gets used to it after a while.'

'You don't *look* tired,' she agreed, thinking he looked more clear-eyed and vital after a short night's sleep than most people did after eight hours plus a lie-in.

'I'm not...but you don't know how much I enjoyed a home-cooked meal and going to bed in a room with some personal touches. Hotel rooms, however *de luxe*, have a terrible sameness about them. The worst part of touring isn't jet lag. It's the feeling of isolation one gets late at night...the loneliness.'

For an instant his blue eyes were bleak. She felt she was glimpsing a side of him he hadn't revealed to her before; a side which appealed to her more than his public image or even his private persona which, up to now, had seemed rather dauntingly self-sufficient. But if he, too, had known loneliness...

Before she could put into words the warm feelings which welled up inside her, Adam said, 'But I came out to get some exercise...not to disturb you. See you later.'

With a lift of the hand he walked on, leaving her irrationally disappointed that he hadn't shown any interest in her sketch or wanted to continue talking to her.

A slight frown contracting her eyebrows, she watched his tall figure lope down the hill and disappear out of sight. But not out of mind.

* * *

After breakfasting with the others, Maggie spent the morning photographing and sketching the Bedales' and Abercorns' houses. There was no need to take measurements, as Diego could give her copies of his conversion plans.

She was in the Bedales' house, rough-sketching a stencil to surround a window Diego had had cut in a thick outside wall, when Adam's voice called from below, 'Are you there, Maggie?'

'Yes... top floor,' she called back.

She heard him bounding up the staircase and then, showing no sign of exertion, he appeared in the doorway. 'Lucinda sent me to ask if you're ready to break for lunch?'

'Yes... in two minutes,' she answered. Then, after a glance at her watch which showed it was five to one, 'But I thought lunch was later in Spain? Two or even three o'clock?'

'It will be two by the time we eat. The Montfalcós have organised a picnic. It will take about an hour to get to the place where we're eating.' His glance went to her feet. 'Lucinda said she could lend you a pair of trainers, but I see you have walking shoes with you.'

'I always bring sensible shoes. High heels are hopeless for travelling or scrambling up ladders and scaffolds, which I quite often have to do. That's also why I tend to wear trousers for work.'

'Having a neat behind, you look very good in them.'

'Thank you.' She tried to take the rather personal compliment in her stride.

But when Adam added, 'Not that one could ever mistake you for a boy,' colour crept into her cheeks. She went on touching up her drawing to avoid meeting his eyes.

'When I asked you what you thought of my house last night, your reaction struck me as tepid,' he said. 'Do I gather it doesn't appeal to you as much as this one and the other place you're going to tackle?'

'On the contrary, I think your house is delightful.'

'But you don't want to design it?'

'I didn't say that.' She had known since she saw the house that, if he pressed her, she wouldn't be able to resist designing the interior for him. 'Tell me about your ideas for it. I hope you have some. I'd rather not have three *cartes blanches* commissions.'

'I have very definite ideas. When we get back from the picnic, I'd like to go round the house with you, explaining them on site.'

'All right, we'll do that.' She began to collect her things together. 'Usually I start by giving people a questionnaire to fill in. Often it makes them think about things they've never considered before. Unfortunately I didn't bring a copy of it with me. I wasn't expecting to meet any of the owners.'

'No problem . . . have it telexed,' he suggested.

'To San Carlos, do you mean? Would a small fishing port have a public telex system?'

'I doubt it, although there's an international oil office there which undoubtedly has one. So does Pobla de Cabres. It was one of Oliver Thornham's priorities. He knew most of the owners would want telex facilities and he pulled strings at ministerial level to get them installed quickly. The teleprinter is in an office next to Diego's. If you call your office immediately, the questionnaire shouldn't take long to come through.'

As soon as Maggie had made her telephone call, they set off in the Pobla de Cabres Range Rover, Diego at the wheel, his wife beside him and the others behind.

Maggie had expected the two men to sit together with Lucinda and herself in the back. Instead she found herself shoulder to shoulder with Adam and sharply conscious of his nearness.

The drive, along rough roads and tracks, eventually brought them to a place where they had to leave the vehicle and, with the men carrying the hamper and cool boxes and the girls bringing the rugs and cushions, go the rest of the way on foot.

The final climb up what had once been a mule-track was worth the effort. It brought them to a turfy plateau with an eagle's view of an *embalse*, a reservoir formed by damming a river.

Soon Diego was pouring champagne while Lucinda unpacked the food and arranged it on a gingham cloth. 'It's a very simple meal,' she warned the others. 'No smoked salmon or plovers' eggs, I'm afraid. If we'd planned this in advance we'd have brought some goodies from Barcelona.'

'Adam may eat them regularly, but I've never had a plover's egg and would rather try local things like those delicious pickled fish you gave us last night,' said Maggie.

'Seconded.' He passed the first glass of champagne from Diego to her, their fingers touching as the glass changed hands. She said, 'Thank you,' and, still looking at her, Adam added, ' "A jug of wine, a loaf of bread—and thou beside me, singing in the wilderness—Oh, wilderness were paradise enow".'

It was said in a light-hearted way, and she took it in that spirit and laughed. But inwardly her heart turned over.

As long as they were with other people, she felt safe. But what if later, while they were going over his house, he tried to flirt with her? Having once succumbed to his charm, she knew herself to be in a weaker position than if he had never kissed her, never held her in his arms.

As matters turned out, she found herself alone with Adam sooner than she had expected. After lunch Lucinda said, 'Would you excuse us for half an hour? We want to ramble around and see if we can find some more mountain irises for our garden.'

'Shall we stretch our legs, too?' Adam suggested, as the others moved off.

He rose to his feet in one supple, continuous movement and held out his hand to her. Had Diego done the same thing, she would have thought nothing of it; but even the most casual physical contact with this man disturbed her equilibrium.

'If you won't think me unsociable, I'd rather stay here and sketch,' she said.

'In that case, I'll take the soft option and have a short siesta.' He dropped back on to the grass, stretching out at full length and crossing his forearms under his head. 'Mm...this is the life,' he murmured, closing his eyes.

Maggie took a small spiral-bound pad and a fibre-tip pen from her bag. She began to draw some strangely shaped crags on the hills beyond the *embalse*. But after a bit, when Adam seemed to be dozing, she turned that page over and started to sketch him.

She had drawn in the long, lean outlines and was starting on the details—the shape of his ribcage under the taut-pulled shirt, and the way his belt buckle lay loosely on a midriff with no ounce of padding between the muscle and skin—when he said suddenly, 'Could you be as happy at Pobla de Cabres as Lucinda appears to be?'

He hadn't opened his eyes and seen her jump and hurriedly cover the unfinished sketch of him with the one of the distant crags.

'I—I don't know,' she said, slightly flustered. 'Would she be happy if she couldn't follow her career here? Possibly not. Have you met their little girl?'

'Yes. Rosa is Diego's daughter by his first marriage. I expect Lucinda will be following Laurian's example and starting a baby herself soon. My impression is that her career as a writer, although important to her, is less important than her marriage. Which is interesting when you consider that she's the daughter of a feminist. Her mother is Georgia Garforth.'

'Really?' Maggie exclaimed. She had seen Ms Garforth on TV, and found it hard to believe that the gentle and obviously domesticated Lucinda was the child of the flamboyant feminist who thought housework a waste of time and husbands an encumbrance.

'I was once on a chat show with Georgia,' Adam went on. 'She's an attractive and witty woman, but too much of a zealot for my taste. Lucinda seems to have inherited her mother's brains, but not her convictions.'

'I remember reading that Admiral Sir Caspar John chose the Royal Navy as his career as a form of rebellion against the undisciplined bohemian life of his artist father, Augustus John,' said Maggie.

As Adam still had his eyes closed and would probably be dazzled by the sunlight for some moments when he opened them, she resumed work on her drawing of him.

'You haven't answered my question. Could you be happy in a place like Pobla de Cabres?'

'Not if it meant giving up my work. I hope to be a wife and mother some day, but not to stop being a designer.'

'That's how Laurian feels,' he said. 'She told me she couldn't have married Oliver if it had meant giving up the fashion business she had established in London because his principal interests were in the Caribbean. Fortunately he was on the point of starting the venture here, so she didn't have to make a choice.'

Something in his tone made Maggie ask, 'Do you disapprove of women putting their careers, if not first, on the same level of importance as the men in their lives?'

'No, it's inevitable they should. But I wonder if Laurian would have found her career rewarding enough to make up for losing Oliver—if no compromise had been possible?' With a sudden swift movement he sat up. 'I think, had it come to the crunch, she would have opted for marriage.'

Having met the Thornhams, Maggie was inclined to agree. 'But I'm sure she would have found some way to continue being herself as well as Oliver Thornham's wife,' she said. 'Marriage ought to be a true merger...not a take-over, don't you think?'

He was considering his reply to that when the others returned, Diego carrying the trug Lucinda had brought with her, in which there were now several of the plants which managed to live and flourish in the thin, parched soil of the mountainsides.

'Instead of wasting water keeping up elaborate gardens of the type you see in the glitzy resorts like Marbella, we're going to encourage the owners at Pobla de Cabres to stick to the plants which are natural to the terrain and need very little watering,' Diego explained. He caught sight of Maggie's sketch of the rocks. 'May I see?'

Reluctantly she surrendered the pad.

'You draw very well. Not all designers and architects do.'

'Thank you.'

As she had feared he might, he looked to see if she had completed more than one sketch and discovered the figure drawing.

'Some of Adam's fans would pay a lot of money for this,' said Diego, with a smile.

'Let me see.' Lucinda peered at the pad. 'Oh, yes…it's *very* good of you, Adam.'

So then Adam got up to look while Maggie remained where she was, trying not to show the embarrassment she felt, although there was no good reason why she shouldn't have made a sketch of him, or of the Montfalcós had they been there while she was drawing.

'I should like to have it myself,' said Adam. 'May I keep it, Maggie?'

Did he really want it, or was he trying to flatter her? The latter seemed the more likely.

'I did it for my assistant, who is one of your fans,' she said. 'You don't mind if I give it to her, do you? Perhaps I should have asked permission to sketch you. I wanted to catch the relaxed pose. I'm afraid I forgot who you were and that you might not like being caught unawares.'

The lines of Adam's mouth hardened. 'What rubbish,' he said brusquely. Then, perhaps aware that his touch had been a touch too scathing for mannerliness, 'I don't care for people creeping up on me with cameras, but this is different. Do what you like with it.'

'Thank you.'

Diego appeared not to notice any undercurrents in this exchange, but Maggie felt sure that Lucinda, with a woman's more sensitive intuition, had picked up every nuance.

When it was time to return to the village, Lucinda suggested that Maggie should sit in front with Diego and Adam in the back with her, confirming that she was aware of friction between them. Maggie wondered what she made of the situation. It must seem odd, to say the least, for an interior designer and a prospective client—who was also a world-class heart-throb—not to be on cordial terms.

They arrived at Pobla de Cabres to find that one of the builder's men had had an accident only a few minutes earlier, not serious but requiring more than first aid. Lucinda said he had better be taken to San Carlos where there was a doctor experienced in treating injuries to men on the off-shore oil rigs when the rigs had been operational.

'I'll come with you,' she said to Diego. 'There's some shopping I want to do. Do you mind being left on your own for a couple of hours, Maggie?'

'Of course not.'

Adam said, 'Maggie and I are going to go over my house. That'll take some time.'

'So you are ... I'd forgotten.'

Lucinda gave Maggie a glance in which there was a hint of uncertainty about leaving them in each other's company. Maggie smiled reassuringly at her.

As the injured man was driven away, she said, 'I'll just fetch my notebook and then I'll join you at your house.'

In the room she was occupying, as well as finding her notebook, she brushed her hair and retouched her lipstick which, with a sun filter lotion and a little mascara, was the only make-up she was wearing.

As she did it, she was aware of the inconsistency of improving her appearance for a man she wanted to keep at arm's length.

Adam was standing in the street outside his house, studying its façade, when she joined him.

'I'm not sure I agree with the decision to keep all the exteriors white,' he remarked. 'It may have been how the village was originally, but I think myself that pastel colour washes could have been more interesting.'

Maggie had already had the same thought. Soft shades of terracotta, ochre, apricot and cream would have been her choice for the village, and on the way back from the picnic she had suggested to Diego that the restrained use of architectural stencils could improve the elevations of one or two of the buildings.

'It wasn't a matter of choice, Diego tells me,' she said. 'The local authorities insisted the village was kept white, although I'm sure that, in the first place, the houses were lime-washed for cheapness, not aesthetic reasons.'

They went inside and she began to question him about his ideas for the house. None of her previous clients had been unmarried men, and it was interesting to compare his responses with those of the wives who had been the dominant voice, at least as far as the design of their houses went, of the married couples she had worked for.

'Nothing pretentious,' said Adam. 'I don't want the place to look as if it has just been done up. I'd rather it looked a bit shabby. It was the lived-in look which caught my eye when I saw the magazine feature on your interiors.'

'I learnt it from Geoffrey Bennison, who specialised in the there-forever look,' she told him. 'Unfortunately he's dead now and I never knew him personally. But I used to study the way he achieved his effects.'

Later, preceding him up the stairs to the spacious multi-level living-room made from six poky bedrooms, Maggie said, 'If you want to furnish with things from your house in Guernsey, I think it's important for me to have a look at the pieces you intend to bring here.'

'You are definitely going to design the house for me, then?'

She drew in a decisive breath. 'Yes, with two other commissions here I can work it in, and I like the house very much. Are you likely to be in Guernsey in the near future?'

'No, but I have a housekeeper who looks after the place for me. She doesn't live in, but she's there almost every day. I'll give you her telephone number. You can fly over for the day or ask Mrs Perelle to book you a room at a hotel across the road. Then you can select what you think will fit in. I'm prepared to rely on your judgement entirely on that score.'

That night Lucinda cooked *albóndigas* for them. These were pork meatballs, casseroled with onions, potatoes and tomatoes. Although Maggie ate meat only when she was a guest, it would have been untrue to say that she didn't enjoy the Spanish dish.

Her questionnaire had come through on the teleprinter, and Adam said he would answer it the next day and post it to her while he was passing through London at the end of the week. However, during the evening there was a telephone call for him.

He took it in Diego's office, rejoining the others to say resignedly, 'No rest for the wicked... I have to go back tomorrow. If your parents are coming here next weekend, Diego, it would save Lucinda the long drive to Barcelona if Maggie flew back with me and your daughter came home with her grandparents. Are you willing to trust your safety to me, Maggie, or would flying with me worry you?'

Flying with him didn't bother her. He couldn't make a pass in mid-air.

'I've never been in a small plane. I'd like to try it,' she answered. 'But will Rosa be upset if you don't come on the day she's expecting you?' she asked Lucinda.

'No, she's perfectly happy staying with my parents-in-law. I'll ring them up in the morning. Going back by air will be more interesting for you, besides being much quicker. It means you can spend the time we would have spent on the *autopista* sunbathing,' said her hostess.

The Apache left the runway and soared into the bright air, giving Maggie an aerial view of the enormous delta surrounding the mouth of the Ebro.

'That little town not far upstream, with the suspension bridge, is Amposta,' Adam told her. 'Further up river you can see the old city of Tortosa. There's a fortified *parador* there where I stayed the first time I came here. The rice fields are dry at the moment, but it won't be long before they're flooded for a new crop. This region is part of the real Spain . . . not an area dependent on tourism.'

Flying at a much lower altitude than on her flight from London was far more interesting, she found. All too soon they were over Sitges, a seaside resort to the south of Barcelona, and Adam was in contact with the control tower at the city's airport.

On a runway reserved for private aircraft, well away from the big jets, he landed the Apache as lightly as a butterfly alighting on a leaf.

When they had taxied to their allotted space and the plane was at a standstill, Maggie said, 'Thank you very much. That was a fascinating experience.'

'The pleasure was mine.' He gave her the smile which always made her pulses quicken.

She had thought that once inside the airport they would say goodbye and go their separate ways, she to return to London in tourist class on a charter flight—she travelled first only on long hauls—and he on one of the scheduled flights.

Now she discovered that, without consulting her, he had booked a first-class seat on her flight and arranged for her to sit with him.

'It seemed the most sensible arrangement, as I can't travel in peace in tourist,' he told her. 'Also it will allow me to go through your questionnaire with you on hand for consultation if there are any points I'm not certain about. You don't mind spending another few hours in my company, do you?'

'Not at all,' she said politely, wishing his arbitrary reorganisation of her travel arrangements didn't fill her with secret pleasure.

Even in the first-class lounge Adam was recognised and watched. Maggie noticed that people stared at her as well, presumably wondering about her connection with him. Perhaps they took her for his secretary.

During the time they spent in the lounge there was never a moment when someone there wasn't staring, either openly or covertly. Maggie began to realise how trying it must be to be famous and subjected to non-stop scrutiny by members of the public. No wonder Adam masked his eyes with dark glasses.

Going out with him in Barbados hadn't prepared her for the attention he attracted in Europe. She was displeased to find that her own reaction to being in a public place with him was, in part, an unworthy pleasure at being seen with him, but mainly a sense of vexation because they were seeing her only as an adjunct to him, not as someone who looked as if she might be interesting in her own right.

She was glad when it was time to board. They were shown to the front of the first-class cabin. Adam insisted on her having the window-seat. The seats across the aisle remained unoccupied, so the only people who could see him were those in the second row of seats, and they were an elderly couple who either didn't know who he was or had been brought up not to stare.

Before they were airborne an *Iberia* stewardess brought them sherry and nuts.

'Excuse me, but I must tell you how much I enjoy your music, Mr Rocquaine.'

'Thank you. I'm glad to hear it.' Adam added something in rapid Spanish which made her dark eyes sparkle. She replied in her own tongue before moving back to serve the people behind them.

Maggie didn't like to ask what he had said to her. Clearly it had been something flattering.

Until lunch was served she looked through the notes she had made, aware that beside her he was dealing briskly with the questionnaire.

They were eating the excellent lunch, each course accompanied by the best Spanish wines, when the captain announced that the Pyrenees were in sight.

'No wonder Spain was cut off from the rest of Europe in the days when people travelled by coach,' said Maggie, peering down at the snow-covered peaks which made a natural frontier between France and Spain.

Adam leaned over the arm of her seat, the better to see the white grandeur of the great mountains.

'When people complain about the quality of modern life, they forget experiences like this...glimpses of places no one ever saw until recently,' he said.

Maggie pressed herself into the outer corner of her seat, giving him maximum access to the spectacular view of untrodden places so high that they would be under snow even in summer.

Although she continued to look at the beauty below them, she was also sharply aware that the last time he'd been as close to her as this had been a few seconds before his fingers had tilted her chin and then slid to the base of her neck, to remain there throughout his first kiss.

The memory of it was almost as dizzyingly potent as the actual kiss had been. As she had that night, she could smell the faint, pleasant scent of him. He didn't seem to use aftershave, but smelt of a combination of clean skin, clean hair and clean clothes which was better than an expensive lotion.

Adam turned his head. Looking into her eyes at close range, he said, 'If we had been making this journey together in the last century, it would have taken weeks, not hours.'

Maggie felt her throat tighten. A vision of travelling more than a thousand miles in his company, sharing all the hazards which such a journey offered then, flashed across her mind's eye and filled her with unwilling longing for that experience.

'Yes,' she said huskily. 'Yes—thank goodness we live in the late twentieth century.'

Adam sat back in his seat. For an instant she thought he looked rebuffed. Just then the pretty stewardess came to refill their glasses and spoke to him in Spanish.

Watching them chatting, Maggie knew she must have been mistaken in thinking her reply had hurt him.

Why should a man who had literally millions of women in thrall care what his interior designer thought of him? His interest in her was confined to her professional skills. She had to remember that.

A car with a driver was waiting for Adam at Heathrow. He insisted on giving Maggie a lift to her office.

'But it's miles out of your way,' she protested.

'I insist.'

She could see that he meant it and didn't argue.

The car was a large Mercedes with a glass partition between the driver and the passengers and darkened glass windows to prevent people seeing who they were.

During the drive into London they discussed some points raised by the questionnaire. It was when they had passed through the West End and were nearing Charterhouse Square that Adam said, 'Will you have dinner with me tomorrow night?'

'I thought you were going to New York tomorrow?'

'Not till the following day.'

Uncertain about the nature of his invitation, Maggie said, 'I—I think we've discussed everything there is to discuss for the time being. There may be some queries arising when you come back from New York.'

'It wasn't the house I wanted to talk about. Do you think we should have a problem finding other things to discuss?' he asked, one eyebrow lifting and a hint of mockery in the line of his mouth.

She averted her eyes from his amused blue ones. 'Possibly not, but I think on the whole it's better not to mix working and social relationships.'

Adam received this in a silence which she found increasingly uncomfortable.

At last he said, 'You're still holding what happened in Barbados against me, aren't you?'

'It has some bearing—yes.'

'Aren't you making a mountain out of a molehill?' he suggested. 'Or should I say, being rather Sabine about a few goodnight kisses? I didn't try to seduce you, if you remember.'

Now within yards of her door, their car was held up by a vehicle badly parked in the narrow street leading to the square. As she looked straight ahead, impatient for the obstruction to be removed, a strong hand curved round her cheek and turned her face towards his.

'Would you have resisted me if I had?' Adam asked shrewdly.

CHAPTER FOUR

HE KNEW, she thought, deeply mortified. He knew as well as she did that, if he had gone on kissing her, anything might have happened. For the first time in her life she had been swept off her feet; and it had been by Adam's choice, not hers, that his final kiss at the gate of Content hadn't led to more passionate embraces inside the house.

Against the cool palm of his hand, Maggie felt her cheeks burning with shame that he knew how close she had come to losing control.

But pride made her hold his gaze and say, with honeyed sarcasm, 'Would any woman? Surely that's why you're called Mr Irresistible? And why I would rather keep our future meetings on a strictly business footing.'

It gave her some satisfaction to see him look even crosser than when Laurian had teased him about the title bestowed on him by one of the tabloids. His hand fell away from her face and some of her fiery blush was reflected in his suntanned cheeks, where the brown skin stretched tautly over the prominent cheekbones which, with the angular jaw and high-bridged nose, gave his face its forceful character.

In the moments that followed, neither of them noticed that the Mercedes had arrived at her address. It wasn't until the driver opened the door on her side that the glare they were exchanging was broken.

Grabbing her shoulder-bag, Maggie scrambled out of the luxurious car on to the pavement.

As Adam followed her, she said frigidly, 'Thank you for the lift,' and looked for her key.

By the time she had unlocked the door, the driver had taken her suitcase from the boot and was waiting to carry it in for her.

'I'll take it up for Miss Hornchurch,' said Adam, extending his hand to take charge of the case.

As the driver was about to hand it over, Maggie grabbed it herself.

'I can manage it, thanks. Goodbye.'

She dived into the hall and closed the door.

By the following morning she had calmed down and was beginning to realise that she should have smiled before she said to him, 'Would any woman?'

That would have been the sophisticated reaction. A flippant answer and a laugh would have made him wonder if he had been mistaken in his assessment of her. The anger underlying her sarcasm must have confirmed his belief that she had been his for the taking.

But only because I had fallen headlong in love with him, she comforted herself, as she ate the chopped fruit and yogurt which was her daily breakfast. And why not? He's a lovable man ... not just in his public image but in his real-life persona. If he were not who he is, maybe something might have come of it. But he isn't an ordinary man; he's an international 'celeb', as PR people say. Why should a man who can have virtually any woman who appeals to him want a woman like me? Except on a temporary basis?

At five minutes past nine, when she knew Alice would have arrived, she telephoned the floor below and told her assistant that she would be working in her flat and didn't want to be disturbed unless it was essential.

'OK, I'll try to leave you in peace. How was your trip?' asked Alice.

'Interesting. I'll tell you about it later . . . probably this afternoon.'

Next Maggie rang up Mrs Abercorn, the wife of the engineer who was working in the Middle East, to make an appointment to visit her later in the week. That settled, she set to work on a scheme for the Abercorns' house.

About ten o'clock the entryphone buzzed. Puzzled, because all mail including parcels was delivered to the studio, Maggie rose from her drawing-table.

'Yes?'

A man's voice with a Cockney accent said, 'Special delivery from Pulbrook & Gould for Miss M Hornchurch.'

'I'll come down.'

Who would send her flowers from what was arguably the best florist's shop in London? she asked herself, as she ran down the four flights of stairs. She could think of only one person.

The flowers had been brought from Pulbrook & Gould's shop in fashionable Sloane Street, miles from Maggie's part of London, by a taxi driver. His cab was parked at the kerb and he was standing on the pavement, clasping a large basket, its contents protected by paper.

'Can you manage it, love?' he asked, as he handed it over.

'Yes, thanks,' she said, with a smile, wondering if she ought to tip him. But she hadn't had the presence of mind to bring some money downstairs with her.

'He must have got it bad . . . and I can see why,' said the driver, who was young, with a cheeky grin.

She couldn't help laughing. 'Thank you . . . goodbye.'

Carrying the basket upstairs, she hoped she wouldn't encounter any of her staff on the way past the third floor. She wondered if there was a note with the flowers.

Luckily no one came out as she passed the door with 'Maggie Hornchurch—Interior Designer' painted on it in the same elegant lettering she had designed for her letter heading and other printed matter.

Back in the privacy of the flat, she placed the basket on her dining-table and carefully removed the paper, revealing a lavish arrangement of white flowers, including sprays of her favourite white lilac, among silver-grey foliage.

It was the most beautiful present she had ever received in her whole life. Even the basket was a lovely one, not the twee gold-painted container supplied by most florists, but a serviceable basket of natural willow. As for the flowers, they were everything she would have expected from a firm supplied by some of the most distinguished gardeners in the land.

Among the flowers was a note. Her fingers a little unsteady, Maggie opened the envelope and took out a card on which, in a bold, clear hand she felt sure was Adam's own, was written the succinct message—'I'm sorry.'

'What did Mrs Abercorn sound like when you spoke to her on the telephone?' asked William.

When Maggie had mentioned her visit to one of the Pobla de Cabres clients, he had insisted on driving her, saying that it would be much quicker than going by train and taxi and he would enjoy a day out, not having had one for some time.

In fact, it had been Maggie's intention to hire a car and drive herself to the rather inaccessible village in

Lincolnshire where her client was living with her daughter. But, having capitulated to William's persuasion, she had to admit it was more enjoyable to be setting out in his company rather than by herself.

'She doesn't sound at all like an invalid,' she told him. 'Her telephone manner was cheerful. She sounded excited at the prospect of going to live in Spain, or perhaps it's more that she misses her husband and looks forward to being reunited with him. I gather she's lived in all sorts of places with him, so it won't be her first time abroad.'

'Why isn't she with him now?'

'I don't know. Her husband is a consultant engineer. Perhaps the project he's working on is somewhere *too* hot for comfort.'

'I don't think my parents have ever spent a day apart since they were married,' said William. 'They have a major wedding anniversary coming up shortly. We're planning a special celebration for them. Dad always takes Mum out to dinner and they wouldn't like that interfered with, but the following weekend we're going to throw a big party for them. Thirty-five years of wedded bliss is a pretty fine achievement, we feel.'

'A marvellous achievement,' she agreed. 'Has it really been bliss all the way?'

'They've had problems and worries like everyone else, but I've never known them to have a big row. Minor spats and some heated arguments . . . but never a serious disagreement. I'd like you to meet them . . . to come home with me that weekend. It would mean sharing a bedroom with my youngest brother's girl. Would you mind that?'

She hesitated. Being taken to meet a man's parents was often thought to mark a significant advance in a relationship. Did William see it in that light, or should she take the invitation at its face value—a chance to share in a happy family occasion?

Wishing she had more time to weigh her answer, she said, 'Not at all. It sounds fun. I'd enjoy meeting your family, William.'

'Good—that's settled, then.'

There was a note of relief in his voice which made her uneasy. Was he reading more into her acceptance than she had intended?

A few days later Maggie attended a buffet luncheon given by a furnishing materials wholesaler to launch a range of chintzes and other fabrics imported from America.

She didn't get back to the studio until late in the afternoon, and was disconcerted to find Adam there, talking to a visibly dazzled Alice. Maggie's heart began to behave like a trapped frog.

He explained his presence by saying, 'Some time ago you told me I didn't know enough about you to commit my Spanish place to you. I hear you live over the shop. If I may... if it's convenient, I'd like to see your place.'

Hoping she looked more composed than she felt, Maggie said, 'Yes, of course... although you know the old saying about the cobbler's children being the worst shod. I've never had time to give my flat the attention I give to my clients' places.'

'Her flat is lovely. Maggie could make a hovel homey,' said Alice loyally.

'You certainly know how to handle staff,' said Adam, a few moments later when he was following her upstairs. 'Obviously they all think very highly of you, especially your senior assistant.'

Maggie unlocked her front door. 'It's mutual. Alice is my right hand. I couldn't cope without her... or the others.'

As she led the way through the tiny hall into her large living-room, she added, 'Your flowers were—and still are—beautiful. Thank you. I would have written a note, but I don't know your address and, not surprisingly, I couldn't find you in the telephone book.'

'No, I have to be ex-directory... but I'll give you my number.' He glanced round the room, saw her telephone with a notepad and pencil pot beside it and went to jot down his number for her. Then he looked round the room again, slowly this time, his eyes scanning her possessions and the way she had arranged them.

'As you can see, I'm an inveterate "snapper up of unconsidered trifles",' she said, with a smile. 'I was buying Paisley shawls and silver photograph frames and Edwardian tablecloths long before they became fashionable. Would you like a cup of tea?'

He nodded. 'Thank you... I would.'

She went to the kitchen and filled and switched on the kettle. Then she slipped across to the bathroom and quickly combed her hair and touched up her light make-up.

The wholesaler's hospitality had been lavish, with a champagne bar alongside the spread of good things to eat. She hadn't drunk as much as many of the guests, and three glasses of champagne weren't as potent as the two strong rum and Cokes she had drunk that unforgettable night at Bella's Place. But Adam himself had a heady effect on her, warping her judgement and clouding her common sense. She knew that while he was here she would have to watch her step.

Why *was* he here? she wondered, returning to the kitchen to set a tea-tray. Did he really want to see her flat? Or was there some other motive behind this unexpected visit?

She was putting biscuits on a plate when he appeared in the doorway. 'May I carry the tray through for you?'

'Thanks. How do you like your tea? Strong, medium or weak?'

'Medium, please... with milk but no sugar. You're a very neat person, I see.' He took in the small, ship-shape kitchen.

'Are you an untidy one?'

Adam shook his head. 'I like things to be orderly. I'm not obsessive about it, but I don't like clutter and muddle. Is that a matter of temperament or upbringing, I wonder?'

'Not upbringing...at least, not in my case. My mother was chronically untidy. It was one of the things which led to her first divorce.'

'And, like Admiral Sir Caspar John, you reacted by becoming a model of neatness.'

She remembered every word of their conversation at the Montfalcós' picnic, but was surprised that he did. She couldn't help feeling pleased that what she had said that day had lingered in his mind.

'Yes, but I also see that my father didn't tackle her untidiness in a sensible way. Instead of losing his temper when she used his electric razor to shave her legs, he should have bought her one of her own. It's easy to see where other people go wrong in their relationships, but perhaps not so easy to be objective about one's own. But I do know I couldn't live with someone who was seriously untidy.'

The tray was ready. Adam moved forward and lifted it from the worktop, but didn't immediately move away. Looking down at Maggie, who was now trapped between him and the sink at the end of the narrow aisle between the units, he said 'You have never lived with anyone...not since you left home, I gather?'

There was an intentness in his gaze which made the question more than a casual enquiry.

'I shared a bedsit with another girl when I was a student, but not since then—no.'

'Don't you ever feel lonely, up here by yourself at night when the rest of the building is empty?'

Disturbed by his closeness, she turned her head to look out of the window at the tops of the trees in the square. It wouldn't be long before new leaves unfurled, veiling the branches with the tender green of spring.

'I feel like a bird nesting in a tall tree. I like being at the top of the building. Is your place in London high up?'

'No, it's somewhere to sleep and keep my working clothes... a small service flat used only as a *pied-à-terre*. If it weren't for the fact that the early morning flights from Guernsey are quite often delayed by fog, even in summer, I wouldn't bother with a base here.'

To her relief he moved away, releasing her from the tension of being within touching distance of him. Even with a tray in his hands, he made her nervous. She couldn't be sure he wouldn't kiss her again, which was something she longed for and dreaded, an uncomfortable state of mind to be in. As she followed him to the living-room, she realised she hadn't been at peace emotionally since the moment she had opened her eyes on the beach in Barbados and seen him looking down at her.

'Where shall I put this?' he asked.

'On the table by the sofa, please.'

The sofa was a three-seater, bought cheaply at an auction, its hideous tight cover now concealed by a striped cotton loose cover. Shared by two people, it left the width of a seat cushion between them.

As he settled his long-boned frame at the other end, Adam said, 'I'm flying out tonight to sing at a private party in Toronto tomorrow. It's one of the few cities I like—very clean and a curious blend of New York-style sophistication and small-town homeliness. It also has the advantage of being on the shore of Lake Ontario, which is so vast it looks like an ocean. I'm sure you'd enjoy working there—if you had time to take on more overseas clients.'

There was a faint twinkle in his eye as he tacked on this final remark.

Maggie handed him his tea. 'Help yourself to a biscuit if you'd like one. Is the person who's giving the party a friend of yours?'

'No, he's one of Toronto's many millionaires who always lays on something special for his wife's birthday. She happens to be a fan of mine. A couple of years ago he wrote saying I could name my fee if I'd sing at her party this year.'

'If that happened to me, I shouldn't know how much to ask. There must be a limit to what even uxorious millionaires will pay to please their wives. How did you decide what to charge?'

'As he's reputed to be close to billionairedom, I felt he could spare a quarter of one of his millions,' Adam said casually, leaning forward to take a biscuit.

Maggie's eyes widened in disbelief. 'And he agreed? He must be mad!'

When his left eyebrow shot up and his mouth took on a quizzical twist, she realised her reaction wasn't exactly complimentary to him.

But it didn't stop her adding indignantly, 'I think that sort of extravagance is shameful. Obviously it's great for you to earn such a colossal amount for a few hours' work, but in a world with so many people in need, it's appalling to spend a fortune of that size on something essentially frivolous. If I were his wife, I couldn't enjoy a treat which had cost so much. A few thousands, yes, OK . . . that's the equivalent to him of a few pounds to me. But a quarter of a million is insane. No performer in the world is worth such a fee.'

Adam was no longer smiling. His expression didn't reveal what he was thinking, but clearly he couldn't be pleased by her condemnatory outburst with its implied criticism of him as well as the rich Canadian.

Meeting his enigmatic gaze, she had the feeling that any second now her association with Adam Rocquaine was going to come to an abrupt end; a prospect which filled her with both terror and relief, the same mixture of conflicting emotions which had bedevilled their relationship from the outset.

Adam placed the biscuit on his saucer and put cup and saucer on the low plate glass table in front of the sofa. She felt sure his next action would be to stride out of the flat and out of her life, pausing only to tell her that if this was how she talked to her clients, he would find himself another designer.

Instead he stayed where he was, saying in a rather odd tone, 'I thought you would say that . . . and of course you're absolutely right. No performer—certainly not I— is worth such a fantastic fee, and I doubt if he would have paid it if I hadn't asked for it to be divided between one of his favourite charities and one of mine. So his wife will be pleased, he will be pleased by her pleasure, and two deserving causes will receive substantial donations.' He paused and smiled at her. 'Does that arrangement meet with your approval?'

Something in his smile brought a flush of warm colour to her cheeks. 'Yes, of course it does ... I'm sorry I flew off the handle like that.'

'I rather hoped you would.'

'You hoped I would? Why?' she asked blankly, unable to follow the workings of his mind.

'Because it confirmed my judgement of your character. It's always gratifying to be proved right, don't you think?'

'But not very gratifying to be judged a hothead,' she said wryly. 'I'm too old to speak my mind without stopping to think first.'

'People who weigh every word before they utter it are too calculating for my taste,' said Adam. 'I don't mind forthright opinions.'

She saw a chance to re-open the conversation from which he had walked away at Barbados airport, leaving her unsure about his relationship with the girl who had been staying there with him.

'Perhaps not, but I shouldn't have jumped to a false conclusion so quickly ... especially not after doing the same thing once before. You told me then I should have asked you about the girl who was with you in the Caribbean. Yet when you mentioned her again, at Laurian's party, I got the impression I had been right in the first place.'

A slight frown contracted his dark eyebrows. 'You were both right and wrong, but there's a reason why I would rather not straighten out that misunderstanding today,' he answered. 'The last time we were together you said it was better not to mix working and personal relationships. For the time being, let's concentrate on our working relationship, shall we? That was what brought me here today. I've had one or two afterthoughts about my answers to your questionnaire. I've jotted them down. As I'm going to be away for some time, it might be as well to go over them with you before I leave.'

He took a folded sheet of paper from the inside pocket of his jacket, opened it and offered it to her. Now even more mystified, Maggie had little option but to defer to his wish not to discuss the other matter at present.

She saw that at the top of the paper he had written his Guernsey address and telephone number and the name 'Mrs Perelle'.

'That's my housekeeper,' he explained. 'I've told her that you'll be coming. Call her when you've decided when to go over.'

It wasn't until he was leaving that he said, 'By the way, did you give your sketch of me to Alice?'

'Why do you ask?' said Maggie, unwilling to admit that she hadn't.

'I felt if you had she would have mentioned it.'

She saw a way to avoid admitting she had kept the drawing for herself. 'Alice has a birthday coming up soon. We'll club together to give her a present—she already has all your records—and I'll give her the sketch then.'

But it won't be the original. I'll have it photocopied, she thought.

'As we've met now, would you like me to write a personal message on it? "Happy birthday, Alice, from Adam" or something similar?' he suggested.

The sketch was in the drawer of her bedside table, but she wasn't about to let him know it was in her bedroom, even. 'What a good idea, but offhand I can't think where I put it. Rather than keep you waiting while I look, why not write on it for her when you come back? You won't be away a month, will you?'

'Not as long as that, no. About ten days, I should think. Goodbye, Maggie. Take care of yourself.' He gave her a businesslike handshake and disappeared down the staircase.

Later, when the others had gone home, Maggie added Adam's afterthoughts to his file on the computer and printed a revised copy which she took up to her flat. But, instead of thinking about his house in Spain, she found herself going over their talk that afternoon, particularly his puzzling reply to her question about his ex-girlfriend. How could her assumption have been both right and wrong? And what possible reason could he have for postponing the explanation of that baffling statement?

I'm in love with him, she acknowledged reluctantly. I'm fond of William and in love with Adam. If only it were the other way around, how much simpler life would be. William is far more suitable. We are two of a kind, with the same objectives in life. Adam is a different species. He fascinates me, but I can't begin to understand him.

Because of complications with her other commitments, it was several weeks before she was able to go to Guernsey. In the meantime, Adam had returned from his trip to Canada and, after a short stay on the island, had gone off again to perform in France and Germany.

He had telephoned her from Guernsey, but their conversation had been strictly business.

By the time Maggie booked her flight to the island, the trees in the square were in leaf and warm weather was forecast.

The flight took an hour in a small, rather noisy aircraft with about thirty people on board. As her taxi was leaving the airport she noticed a great many private aeroplanes parked inside the perimeter fence. They reminded her of the flight to Barcelona with Adam. Where was he now? There wasn't an hour in the day when she didn't think of him, she realised.

The road to St Peter Port was lined with modern bungalows, much older granite cottages and a number of hotels. Maggie noticed that several bungalows had flowers and produce for sale at their gateways.

Soon the buildings proliferated and she realised they must be on the outskirts of the island's main town. But even here there was a countrified atmosphere, with cows grazing in a small field between built-up areas.

Further on, the houses became larger and more elegant with Regency and early Victorian architecture predominating and fine old trees shading large gardens. Suddenly, where the road began to slope downhill and was overhung by a magnificent copper beech and two live-oaks, the driver swung into the forecourt of a tall, colour-washed house with basement windows on a level with the taxi's wheels and two flights of steps rising to a front door at the side.

Maggie climbed out and looked up at the façade of Adam's childhood home. On each of the three main floors was a pair of many-paned Georgian windows with internal shutters and lined curtains with fringed pelmets.

She was mounting the steps to ring the bell when the front door opened and a neatly dressed woman in her sixties appeared. Having introduced herself as Mrs Perelle, she ushered Maggie through an outer hall, with glazed doors giving a glimpse of a long stone-walled garden at the rear, to an inner front door leading into a spacious hall from which rose a wide staircase.

'The drawing-room and dining-room are down here, but they haven't been used for a long time. The room Mrs Rocquaine liked best is upstairs on the first floor. That's where she had her embroidery frame and Mr Adam his piano. I'll show you,' said Mrs Perelle.

On the second flight of stairs she paused to pick up some petals which had fallen from a vase of flowers on the window-sill.

'Which island is that?' asked Maggie, looking at the view of neighbouring gardens, the sea and beyond it another island.

'That's Sark,' the housekeeper told her. 'They don't allow cars there, only tractors. It's a pity there isn't some restriction on traffic here, if you ask me. Not many years ago the visitors rented bicycles to look round Guernsey. Now most of them hire a car. But walking is the best thing to do here. There are some lovely walks. It's a shame you're only staying one night, Miss Hornchurch.'

By now they had reached the first floor, where she opened a door leading into a large sunlit room with windows at either end.

'I thought you'd like coffee and a biscuit before I show you the rest of the house,' said Mrs Perelle. 'Have a look round this room while I make the coffee.'

Left on her own in the spacious, high-ceilinged room, Maggie went first to one of the windows overlooking the garden. It was flanked by other long gardens, all surrounded by high granite walls supporting fruit trees and climbing shrubs. Close to the second south-facing window was a comfortable chair, and near it a standing embroidery frame on which was stretched an unfinished piece of canvas work. In what had once been a shallow cupboard and was now a recess housing books and antique work-boxes, most of the books were on subjects relating to needlework.

At the other end of the room the emphasis was on music. Here stood a large grand piano, and here the alcoves made by converting some more shallow cupboards were filled with a musician's reference library.

The view from this side of the room was of an ornate building with mock battlements and a quatrefoil-pierced parapet above its pillared veranda. A discreet sign, 'Grange Lodge Hotel—Fully Licensed' was painted on the glass light above the door.

'That's where you'll be staying tonight,' said the housekeeper, coming back to find Maggie still looking at the hotel. 'You could have spent the night here, but Mr Adam thought you might not like being on your own. I don't live in, you see. They'll make you very comfortable at the hotel.'

'What an unusual building. Do you know how old it is?' asked Maggie.

'It was built about 1830 for Charles de Jersey, the King's Attorney General . . . so Mr Adam told me. He's interested in history,' said the housekeeper. 'All I can tell you about it is that during the Occupation it was the Gestapo's headquarters. I wasn't here in those bad times. I was born on the mainland and came over when I married. A very quiet place it was then, just after the war. There's more going on here nowadays, but we're still a bit behind the times—which is all to the good, in my opinion. Mr Adam is always glad to get back, and he should be a good judge. He's been everywhere there is to go.'

'Have you known him all his life?' Maggie asked, sitting down on a sofa with a low table in front of it on which Mrs Perelle had placed the tray.

'Nearly all his life. He would have been about seven when I started to work for Mrs Rocquaine. Very tall for his age even then, he was.'

Having poured out two cups of coffee and invited Maggie to help herself to cream and sugar, Mrs Perelle rose from the other end of the sofa and crossed the room to a table on which stood a number of silver-framed photographs. Selecting two, she brought them back with her.

'This was taken on his fifteenth birthday. His grandmother was a tall woman, but he was a good head taller.' She handed one photograph to Maggie.

It showed a white-haired but still very handsome old woman arm in arm with a gangling schoolboy in cricket whites. The two of them were sharing a joke, he grinning down at her, she smiling lovingly up at him while someone snapped them standing under the myrtle tree Maggie had noticed in the garden.

'This is about five years later.' Mrs Perelle passed her the second photograph.

It was a shot of three people, two young men with a girl standing between them. All were smiling at the camera and there was something about them which brought the expression *jeunesse dorée*—gilded youth— into Maggie's mind. Perhaps it was because all three were exceptionally good-looking and dressed for a special occasion: the men in morning suits and the girl in a chiffon dress with a wide-brimmed straw hat in her hand.

'That was taken at a big wedding,' said the house-keeper. 'The other young man, Guy Vazon, was Mr Adam's best friend.'

'Who was the lovely girl?' Maggie looked at the oval face framed by silky fair hair, and wondered what it was like to be as beautiful as that.

'Elizabeth Fermain...as she was then. Elizabeth Vazon now...widowed at twenty-five. Mr Guy was killed and she was badly hurt when he crashed his Ferrari in France. Drove like the devil, he did, even here on the island. It's a wonder he didn't get killed, or kill someone else, long before. She's all right again now. She's recovered her health. But she isn't the wild girl she was. A thing like that changes people. It upset Mr Adam for months. Like brothers, he and Mr Guy were. Not a bit alike in their ways, but devoted to each other. "Thank heavens Adam wasn't with them," Mrs Rocquaine said to me, when she heard about the accident. They were almost inseparable, those three. Even after the other two got married, they still went on holidays together.'

How strange, was Maggie's private thought. One wouldn't expect a young married couple to want anyone tagging along, not even their closest mutual friend. Nor could she understand why Adam should want to make up a trio. A quartet which included his current girlfriend might have been feasible, but not the proverbial crowd of three.

'How sad—to be widowed so young,' she said. 'Did they have any children?' They didn't sound the sort of couple who would have started a family early in their marriage.

The housekeeper confirmed this impression with a shake of the head. 'Just as well, in the circumstances. Mr Guy was always a spendthrift, even as a teenager.

The debts he left when he was killed didn't surprise anyone who knew him. Luckily for Elizabeth, Mr Adam settled them all—and paid her hospital bills. Generous to a fault, he is.' She gave Maggie a searching look. 'In any deserving cause. But he won't be taken for a ride. It's not "easy come, easy go" with him as it was with Mr Guy. Mr Adam never wastes money, and he expects good value for what he does spend.'

'Quite right...so do I,' Maggie said firmly, amused by this pointed warning that she shouldn't attempt to overcharge him for her services.

She took the fact that the housekeeper had confided some fairly intimate details of his background to her as a sign that Mrs Perelle was lonely looking after a house whose owner was often away.

Perhaps feeling that she might have been indiscreet, the older woman started talking about the weather, and didn't refer to her employer again until she was showing Maggie the rest of the house.

Adjoining the first-floor sitting-room was a small room containing Adam's record and cassette library. On the same floor, at the front of the house, was a modern kitchen installed as a replacement for the old-fashioned kitchen and sculleries down in the basement.

On the second floor was the late Mrs Rocquaine's bedroom, overlooking the garden, two other bedrooms and a bathroom unchanged since Victorian times, except that modern heating had been added to it.

Adam slept in one of the two rooms at the very top of the house. From his bay-shaped dormer window all the islands except Alderney were visible. Mrs Perelle pointed out the distant outline of Jersey, the largest Channel Island, and also, within a short boat-trip from St Peter Port, little Herm and even smaller Jethou.

The other room on this floor was a box-room full of ancient cabin trunks and heavy leather suitcases, relics of a time when travellers could rely on porters to handle their luggage. From the window in here, Alderney could be seen.

'The best view is from the roof,' said the housekeeper, indicating a flight of wooden treads leading to a trap-door. 'I've never been up there myself . . . I've no head for heights. But Mr Adam often goes up there in summer. Now I'd better get on and leave you to look round at your leisure. There's a lot more furniture stored in the basement . . . things his parents bought on their travels or things he's taken a fancy to on his. You've plenty to choose from for his new place in Spain.'

Left to her own devices, Maggie couldn't resist re-turning to Adam's bedroom to look more closely at it. It was completely unlike the bedrooms of other stars and showbiz personalities she had seen featured in maga-zines. Here was no kingsize divan extravagantly draped, no carpeted dais, nothing trendy or glitzy.

The attic room, with its breathtaking seascape views to the east, showed clearly that it had once been a schoolboy's lair which had gradually evolved into a man's room.

Both the brass bedstead and the shabby leather chesterfield were originals, not modern copies. An old telescope mounted on a tripod stood by the window, and a sturdy smoker's bow chair at a somewhat battered pedestal desk was doubtlessly where Adam had once done his homework.

Shortly before one o'clock, Mrs Perelle suggested that Maggie might like to go across to the hotel and see her room there before coming back for the light lunch the housekeeper had prepared for them both.

'What a pity you can't stay a few days,' she said again, while they were eating it at a drop-leaf table in the sitting-room.

'I thought I might stretch my legs and have a quick look round St Peter Port after lunch,' said Maggie. 'Then, if you've no objection, I'll come back and carry on here till the hotel serves dinner.'

'You'll be on your own after half-past four,' the housekeeper warned her.

'I shan't mind that. It's not an eerie house. If there are any ghosts here, I'm sure they're all benign ones,' Maggie answered, smiling.

She returned from her walk into town longing to have more time to explore the steep streets with their French names—Le Grange, Vauvert and Allez Street were three she had noticed—and to watch the comings and goings in the castle-guarded harbour.

Before she went to bed that night she had made up her mind that she would postpone her return by twenty-four hours.

By the evening of her second day in Guernsey, Maggie had selected the furniture most suited to the house in Spain and had no good reason to delay going back to London—except that the longer she stayed on the island the better she liked it, and it was a long time since she had had a holiday, apart from the brief busman's holiday at Pobla de Cabres.

She had returned to the house, after dining at the hotel, and was in the sitting-room, reading, when she heard sounds from below. Thinking it must be Mrs Perelle—though why she should come back at this hour Maggie couldn't imagine—she waited for her to come up to the first floor.

But it wasn't the housekeeper who presently appeared in the doorway.

'Hello...I didn't expect to find you here,' said Adam.

'I didn't expect to see you, either,' she answered, aware that her traitorous heart was turning somersaults with excitement at his unexpected arrival. 'Mrs Perelle said you wouldn't be back till the week after next.'

'The best laid plans...et cetera. When did you arrive?'

'Yesterday morning. I've a seat on the mid-afternoon flight back tomorrow.'

'Would you do me a favour?' he asked. 'Put the kettle on while I run this stuff up to my room.'

He was holding a grip in one hand, the fingers of his other hand being hooked round the handle of a suit-bag hanging down behind his left shoulder.

'Of course. Which would you like? Tea or coffee?'

'Tea, please, and a couple of slices of *gâche* if there's any going. Has Mrs P introduced you to Guernsey's speciality?'

'Yes, and I find it very more-ish,' said Maggie, having sampled the island's fruit loaf the previous afternoon and again at teatime today.

By the time Adam reappeared she had made a pot of tea and cut and buttered some *gâche* for him.

'I see you've found Brett's book on all the old buildings in the town,' he remarked with a glance at the book she had put aside on first seeing him.

'Yes, and I've looked at Bonamy House and Lukis House,' she said, referring to two fine houses she had paused to admire on her way to the port. 'I only wish there were time to see all the buildings he mentions as being outstanding.'

Adam was pouring himself a cup of tea. 'Can't you make time? Must you return to London tomorrow? I'd like to show you some of my favourite places.'

'It's kind of you, but I have commitments which I can't shelve. At least there'll be time to discuss the choice of furniture for Pobla de Cabres with you.'

'Yes, although I may not be up early tomorrow,' he said, relaxing his tall frame in the manner of someone who has been continuously on the go for a long time. 'I've had a succession of short nights. I don't feel tired at the moment, but when I do go to bed I shall probably sleep round the clock. Are you comfortable across the road?'

'Very, thank you. They've given me a room overlooking the garden which is full of bluebells at the moment. It's time I was getting back. Do you mind if I take the Brett book with me?'

'Not at all, but don't run away yet. Guernsey is supposed to be behind the times, and a hotbed of gossip, but people aren't so strait-laced that our being alone in the house at this decorous hour will cause talk. If you're not having tea, let me get you a drink.'

As he would have risen from the sofa, she forestalled him by saying quickly, 'No, thank you . . . but that reminds me—I said I would have a drink with an old lady who's staying at the hotel after she had seen a television series she's following. She'll be wondering where I am.'

The excuse was genuine. She had said that, if she returned to the hotel in time, she would join the elderly Yorkshirewoman who was staying there with her daughter and son-in-law.

Adam insisted on seeing Maggie not only to the door but across the main road, although there was little traffic on it at this time of night. Four times a day an almost continuous stream of vehicles flowed up and down the hill during the island's rush hours. Because it was only a ten-minute drive from one side of Guernsey to the other, many workers went home for lunch.

Observing their cheerful faces and the easy-going manner with which they gave way to other motorists emerging from side roads and gateways, Maggie had felt that, even with the build-up of traffic of which Mrs Perelle complained, the pace of life here was still leisurely and unstressful compared with London.

When she went to her room an hour later, after a chat with the old lady, Maggie wondered if it would be madness to allow Adam to persuade her to prolong her stay. But perhaps as she had declined the suggestion quite firmly this evening he wouldn't mention it again.

When she turned out her light, she still hadn't made up her mind what she would say if he did put it to her a second time.

The following morning, before the shops in St Peter Port opened and while cars were still bumper to bumper in Le Grange, Maggie walked down the hill, pausing to look in the windows of an antique shop on the opposite side of the road from the extraordinary Tudor-revival architecture of Elizabeth College, Adam's old school.

On her first walk into town she had noticed a branch of Next in the sett-paved High Street and a Benetton further along. Although she knew she was behaving more like a love-sick teenager than a level-headed career woman in her middle twenties, it was her intention to buy a few extra clothes just in case Adam did urge her to postpone her flight back a second time.

Next was a chain of shops whose simple styles and classic accessories were very much on her wavelength.

From the summery clothes on the rails, she picked out a T-shirt, long shorts and a cotton dress. Upstairs she found a pair of shoes to supplement the penny loafers she had thought would see her through her short visit to the island.

By the time she walked back up steep Smith Street, feasting her eyes on the lacy Victorian cast-iron decorating some of the façades, she was laden with several carriers, including a shocking pink bag containing some duty-free scent and cosmetics from Le Riches, some for herself and some for Alice and the other girls.

To her surprise, the receptionist at the hotel greeted her with the news that Adam had telephoned half an hour earlier. He would like to talk to her as soon as she got back from her walk.

Maggie ran up to her room to put away her shopping. She thought it unlikely that Adam would have been looking out of his north-facing windows and seen her enter the hotel. If he had, the contents of the carriers were easily explained as presents for friends.

In the outer hall of his house, Mrs Perelle was arranging flowers in a bowl on the table.

'As it's such a lovely morning, Mr Adam is having breakfast in the garden,' she told Maggie.

He was reading a newspaper as she walked along the path between the herbaceous border and the lawn. A conservatory had been built against the high granite wall at the end of the garden and Adam had brought out some of the outdoor furniture stored there. He was lying on a cushioned chaise-longue with a wheel underneath it at one end and handles projecting from the other. On a low table beside it was his breakfast tray, and he had put out a comfortable cane armchair with a leg-rest upholstered in the same green and white canvas.

He rose when he saw her coming. 'Good morning.'

'Good morning. You didn't sleep late, after all?'

'The sun woke me up. They're forecasting an early heatwave. Forget about going back to London. Come and picnic with me on the cliffs. Call your office and tell them you'll be back when the weather changes.' He had already tossed the newspaper aside. Now he stepped forward and took both her hands in his. 'Life is for living, Maggie. Guernsey in spring, when the sun shines, is like nowhere else in the world. You musn't miss this chance to see the island at its best.'

How could she say no? She didn't. Withdrawing her hands from his light clasp, she nodded. 'All right. I'll stay... till tomorrow.'

By mid-morning they had been through the list of furniture she thought suitable for the Spanish house, and Mrs Perelle had been down to the fish market and brought back some fresh crabmeat to make into Adam's favourite crab and cucumber sandwiches.

By noon they were standing on a path high above the calm, shimmering sea which, where it lapped the rocks of a small inaccessible cove a hundred feet or more below their vantage point, was the colour of an emerald and as clear as glass.

'Beautiful, isn't it?' said Adam, surveying the scene around them and speaking with a note of proprietorial pride in his voice. He had changed into shorts and sandals and was carrying their lunch in a light rucksack strapped to his broad shoulders.

'Heavenly,' Maggie agreed, inhaling a deep breath of air which mingled the sharp tang of ozone with the country scents of warm turf and wildflowers.

'There are cliffs all along this south coast. The north of the island is flat with wide, open bays instead of these coves and inlets,' he told her, before continuing along the path which now wound its way through tall thickets of gorse and bracken.

Where the land formed deep ravines, flights of steps led up and down and Adam's long sun-burned legs sprang lightly up the ascents at a pace which she found it hard to match.

'Am I going too fast for you?' he asked, pausing half-way up the steepest climb so far.

'Yes,' she admitted, laughing, glad to catch her breath for a moment.

'It's not far now to our lunch place. Then you can stretch out and relax.' He resumed the climb, but more slowly.

Their destination was a promontory at a level between the tops of the cliffs and the sea. Huge boulders of granite formed natural back-rests, and the rabbit-nibbled turf was warm under Maggie's bare calves as she stretched out her legs and gave a long sigh of pleasure at the heat of the sun and the beauty of the rugged coastline.

'There don't seem to be many other people about,' she said, while Adam was unpacking the rucksack.

'Even in summer, the cliff paths are never crowded. At this time of year you can walk all day and not pass more than a handful of people.' He handed her a glass of wine. 'And very few visitors to the island discover the paths which network the interior.' Now he was offering her an open packet of sandwiches.

'Thanks.' The strenuous walk from where he had left his car had sharpened her appetite. She savoured a mouthful of wine and then bit, with relish, into a sandwich. 'Mm...this crab is delicious.'

Adam settled himself comfortably beside her. 'I used to come here with my grandmother as a small boy. It was one of her favourite places. She was an active old bird. We tramped all over the island together and she told me its history and its legends—of which there are dozens. It was...still is a great place to grow up.'

Suddenly his expression changed. For a second or two he looked troubled. She wondered if speaking of his boyhood had brought back memories of his best friend, Guy Vazon, now buried somewhere in France unless his remains had been brought back to the island.

To distract him from possibly painful recollections, she said, 'Tell me some of the legends.'

'Some other time. I want to hear about you. You say very little about yourself.'

She gave a slight shrug. 'My childhood wasn't a happy time. I began to enjoy life when I started standing on my own feet.'

'Very nice feet,' said Adam, looking at them. On arrival she had slipped off her loafers to expose her slim feet to the sun. 'Everything about you is pleasing,' he went on. 'I thought so the first time we met.'

'Thank you.' His praise and the quality of his smile warmed her heart as pleasurably as the sun was warming her skin.

'In my experience it's rare to meet someone one likes in every respect,' he continued. 'In fact, it's never happened to me before. I've met pretty girls and clever girls and girls who were fun to be with, but never a girl who combined all those qualities—and several others besides.'

Maggie didn't know what to say. There was a considerable pause before she decided that, 'I like you

very much too,' was the most suitable reply to his unexpected encomium.

But as she started to speak Adam cut in with,
'Sorry...I forgot for a moment that you like to keep
your clients at arm's length. Have another sandwich.'
He offered her the packet.

She took one, realising as she did so that she had completely lost her appetite for food. What she wanted more
than anything at this moment was not to keep Adam at
arm's length, but to have him take her in his arms and
kiss her the way he had kissed her in Barbados.

CHAPTER FIVE

'I HOPE I haven't tired you out,' said Adam, unlocking the car.

After their picnic they had continued along the cliff path for about two miles, returning to their starting point by way of various inland footpaths.

'Not a bit. I thoroughly enjoyed it,' she said truthfully. 'I do a lot of rushing about in London, but it isn't the same as walking in the country...especially in this marvellous air. I feel invigorated, not tired.'

'It's a pity we can't go around on bikes any more,' he said, on the way back. 'But it's not fun, or safe, any more with so many cars on the road. For tonight I've booked a table at a restaurant overlooking the harbour. It's a favourite haunt of French yachtsmen who sail over here at weekends, so although the service is formal the customers aren't. Seamen's sweaters are quite in order. You needn't worry about not having anything suitable to wear.'

Remembering how their last night out together had ended, Maggie felt her pulses quicken. If the sky stayed clear tonight, would they stroll up the hill from the town as they had strolled on the beach? Would he kiss her goodnight...and perhaps, this time, not walk away?

The late afternoon increase in traffic had begun on the main road leaving the town when they reached St Peter Port. Adam parked the car in his forecourt and saw Maggie across the busy road. Being in the middle of a discussion about the bathrooms in his Spanish house, he came inside the hotel with her and was there when the receptionist handed Maggie her key.

'You've just missed a telephone call from London, Miss Hornchurch. Mr William Bramshott rang up about five minutes ago. I wrote down his name and number. He wanted to know when you were going back to the mainland. I said as far as we knew you were leaving tomorrow.'

'William Bramshott? Isn't that the chap who was with you at Laurian's dinner party?' Adam enquired.

'He gave me a lift there and ran me home—yes,' she agreed.

Whatever was in Adam's mind as he looked thoughtfully at her remained unspoken. He said only, 'I'll come over for you about seven. We'll have a drink at La Frégate on the way down. You may not approve of their décor but they have magnificent views from the bar and dining-room. See you later.'

Was she imagining that he looked slightly put out? Maggie wondered, as she watched him re-crossing the road.

In her room she undressed and ran a bath. Relaxing in the warm water, she realised that she *was* drowsy. Maybe a nap on the bed was a good idea. She had better arrange for the receptionist to call her at six-thirty. It wouldn't do to oversleep. She needed at least half an hour to do her face and dress.

'How is the weather in London?' Adam asked, as they walked into town by a different way from the two she knew.

'I have no idea,' said Maggie.

'You didn't speak to Bramshott?' he asked, raising an eyebrow.

She shook her head. In fact, she had dialled William's office number but got no reply. She hadn't tried his home number.

The fact that Adam had asked made her feel, for the first time, that he was as uncertain of her feelings as she was of his. He had met William. He knew that he wasn't in the same league as himself as far as looks went. Yet she sensed that he wasn't pleased about William's call.

After drinks at the hotel with the panoramic view of the other islands, they descended to harbour level and soon were installed at a window table in a restaurant overlooking the crowded yacht marina.

'When are you thinking of going to Pobla de Cabres again?' Adam asked, when they had finished deciding what to eat.

'Fairly soon, I think.'

'I'm hoping to get down there myself at the end of the month. Would you care to try a longer flight with me?'

At lunchtime she had hesitated to respond to his overture. This time her reaction was immediate.

'I'd like that very much, Adam—if we don't have conflicting commitments. I enjoyed my first flight as your passenger enormously. What about the Pyrenees? Can a small plane go over them?'

'No problem. The peaks you saw when we crossed the Pyrenees together were some of the highest. I've flown through the passes and also followed the coastline. It takes considerably longer than going with an airline, you realise, but if we start out in good time we can lunch in the south of France and be at the village by teatime. Good weather is the crucial factor. I wouldn't take you if there was any risk of it being bumpy.'

'Are bumps much worse in a small plane?'

'I should think they must be, for a passenger. A small plane doesn't feel as solid as a larger one and most people, very naturally, have more confidence in a professional pilot.'

'If I didn't have total confidence in your capabilities as a pilot, I wouldn't fly with you,' she said quietly, meeting his eyes.

As usual he was wearing tinted glasses which, suddenly, he removed and slipped inside his top pocket.

'Good, I'd like you to have total confidence in me, period. But I don't think you do...not quite...not yet.'

The intensity of his gaze made Maggie catch her breath. But, as an impetuous denial of his statement trembled on her tongue, the wine waiter came to the table, apologetic for having kept Adam waiting.

And by the time the question of what to drink was settled she had thought better of that declaration. For wasn't he right? Wasn't there still a lingering element of doubt in her mind, even though her heart no longer had any reservations?

It wasn't late when they climbed the steep granite steps from the quay to the high street and returned to the top of the town under a still cloudless sky from which an almost full moon hung like a white paper lantern.

When Adam invited her in for coffee, Maggie didn't demur. She would have been disappointed if he hadn't.

By night, lit by large table-lamps which shed light where it was needed and left the rest of the room in a restful half-light, the big room on the first floor was even more welcoming and peaceful than during the day.

Adam closed the shutters on the street side so that people in the hotel across the road couldn't see in, but he left the shutters on the garden side open.

'Let's have some music,' he said, opening a section of his record library. 'Your taste in music is one of the many things I don't yet know about you, Maggie. I remember your telling me that you were a visual rather than aural person. But there must be some music you like.'

At an earlier stage of their relationship she would have expected him to have something soft and smoochy laid on, so that at the touch of a button a romantic song—possibly one of his own—would add to the seductive atmosphere.

'I'm beginning to share Alice's taste for your music. How about "Daydreams"?' she suggested, naming one of his most successful singles.

He shook his head, selecting a record whose sleeve she couldn't see from where she was standing, close to one of the garden windows. A few moments later she recognised the first soft notes of something by Chopin. The *étude* or sonata—she knew the music without knowing its name—was the perfect aural accompaniment to the visual delight of the moonlit walled garden, a distant glimpse of silver sea and the dark outline of Jersey on the horizon.

Adam came to stand behind her. 'I'll make some coffee in a minute.'

As she had in the restaurant earlier, when he took off his glasses and gave her that deep, intent look, Maggie found herself holding her breath. Every instinct told her that the moment had come when he was going to touch her, hold her...

He put his hands lightly on the curves of her shoulders. 'But first——' He turned her to face him. 'I must do what I've wanted to do all evening...' he looked down at her for a long moment '...which is this.' His hands glided down her back to draw her against him, and he bent his head to kiss her.

We are not strangers, you and I.

As she had on that other night in Barbados, she surrendered herself to the mastery of his arms and lips. Had they kissed in other places, other lives? It seemed so natural, so familiar to be crushed against his powerful body, her head cupped by the palm of his hand as his warm mouth worked its potent magic on her senses.

A long time later he relaxed his hold on her slightly. Speaking into her hair, he said huskily, 'After that, do you need telling in words how I feel about you...darling Maggie? May I take it you feel the same?'

'I felt almost like this a long time ago...in Barbados. But the next day it seemed that you had only been fooling with me.'

'I was never more serious in my life. Unfortunately, at that time, I was involved with someone else. If it hadn't been for that fact, I wouldn't have kissed you goodnight at the garden gate. I'd have stayed talking to you all night and the next day we'd have been married by special licence. Within an hour of our meeting that evening, I knew you were the girl I'd been waiting for all my life.'

She drew back a little. 'But you must have felt that about the other girl once...mustn't you?'

'No...never. You are the first and only woman I have loved. I don't count a few youthful infatuations while I was still immature. Everyone goes through that phase. It's a necessary part of growing up. To explain why I was living with someone for whom I felt no more than affection is rather a complicated story which I think I had better explain now.'

'I wish you would. It's been a puzzle and a worry to me for so long.'

Adam released his hold on her and moved away to the table on which stood the photograph Mrs Perelle had shown her on the day of her arrival.

'I don't know whether you've noticed this,' he said, bringing it to her. 'The other people in it are my best friend, Guy Vazon, who is dead now, and Elizabeth Fermain, the girl he was in love with and eventually married. At the age of twenty I was quite smitten with her too. She was by far the prettiest girl on the island, and a lot of young men were crazy about her. She was an accomplished flirt and kept us all on a string. Then I spent a year back-packing my way round the world, and by the time I got back I'd met a lot of girls who weren't pretty but had more durable qualities such as a sense of humour, kindness, integrity. Elizabeth had lost her hold on me, but not on Guy. He was still mad about her.'

'Didn't he go away anywhere?' Maggie enquired. 'I should have thought most young people who had grown up here would want to see other places, if only the mainland.'

'Guy did go away. He wanted to go to Oxford or Cambridge and he had the brains to make it, but he was lazy and didn't work hard enough, so he had to settle for a place at one of the red-bricks. For a time he had a lot of girlfriends, but he was never serious about anyone except Elizabeth. When they married, some people said they were ideally matched. Others felt it was a disaster. Guy didn't have to work. He'd inherited money from his maternal grandfather and Elizabeth had a generous allowance from her father who also bought them their house. For three years their life together was a non-stop party, either here or somewhere where jet-setters congregate.'

'Did you spend much time with them?'

He nodded. 'Guy and my grandmother were the two people I cared about most. I wanted to see him doing something more purposeful than roar around Europe in a fast car, soaking up *vino* and sun and leading the life of a playboy. Fortunately for me I wasn't with them when he ran out of road. Elizabeth was terribly injured and probably wouldn't have recovered as well as she has if her father hadn't called in the top man in orthopaedics to supervise her treatment. Then, just when she was pulling round physically if not mentally, he had a fatal heart attack. After that she was in a bad way emotionally for a long time...on the brink of a nervous breakdown.'

'How terrible to lose her father so soon after losing her husband,' Maggie said, shocked.

'Yes, if life had been too easy for her up to that point, it certainly dumped a load of troubles on her that year,' Adam said, frowning. 'I did what I could to see her through it. Our grief over Guy was a bond we hadn't had before. When she asked if she could come with me on a trip to America, I didn't foresee it would lead to a closer relationship. But Liz is a beautiful woman and I was never cut out to be a monk. Perhaps it's hard for you to understand how it happened. I can only tell you that, at the time, it seemed a better idea than the alternative...casual relationships with people we didn't care about. If we didn't have a great deal in common in other ways, at least we both came from the same place and had, in effect, the same past. That, and our memories of Guy, helped to mask all the things which were lacking.'

Adam took her by the hand and led her to the sofa. When they were sitting down, he clasped both her hands in his long strong fingers and said, 'The French have an expression: *"faute de mieux"*. As you probably know it means "for want of something better". That's what the relationship with Elizabeth was. Perhaps that's hard for you to understand, but try to imagine yourself being some years older than you are now and still looking for the right man. Might you not be tempted to settle for a workable substitute?'

Before she could answer, he went on, 'There's another aspect to the situation I was in. Any singer—certainly of popular music and probably of grand opera as well— attracts fans. You must have heard stories of pop stars picking out girls from a crowd of eager groupies... girls they'll discard as casually as empty cigarette packets?'

Maggie nodded.

'Most of my fans aren't besotted to that extent, thank heavens,' said Adam, with a grimace. 'But there are quite large numbers of women who become infatuated with actors and TV performers. They're in love with the image, not the reality, but they write letters and some-times go to amazing lengths to meet their idols. Often they're attractive women whom you wouldn't expect to be willing to jump into bed with a stranger. But they are, and there used to be times when I was tempted to take what was on offer. Hotel rooms in foreign cities where one doesn't have any real friends can be lonely places, believe me.'

'I'm sure they are,' she agreed. 'I've been lonely in my own flat. Life is lonely when you have no one to share it with... I understand that very well.'

'Then can you also understand how Elizabeth and I drifted into a partnership which wasn't what either of us wanted but was better than nothing?'

'Yes, I understand that too, Adam. What worries me is that she may have developed deeper feelings for you than you did for her. How do you know she didn't fall in love with you while you were together?'

'I know Elizabeth very well. Frankly, I don't think she's capable of love in your definition of the term. Her feelings for Guy had a lot to do with his looks and his daredevil style. To be brutally honest, she was more upset by the ending of their way of life than by losing Guy himself. She certainly wouldn't have joined forces with me if I'd still been back-packing and staying in cheap hotels,' he said drily.

When Maggie's expression continued to reflect uncertainty, he let go her hands and took her face between his palms.

'Darling girl, don't look so troubled. Elizabeth isn't heartbroken, I promise you. Probably by now she's found someone else whom she much prefers to me. I wasn't by any means an ideal companion in her eyes. We'd no sooner arrived in Barbados than we had a major row. On the plane flying out there were some people who have a house at Fort George. It's a building development to the south of St Peter Port. Some extremely nice people live there, but it has the reputation of being an enclave of *nouveaux riches* and I have to say I've met some Fort Georgers whose conversation does consist of boasting about their worldly possessions. I didn't want to go nightclubbing with her cronies, and Elizabeth didn't want to explore the island's back roads in the moke. So she took herself off to another room and sulked, hoping it would bring me round.'

'Your housekeeper told the housekeeper at Content that Mrs Vazon had a migraine.'

'It would have worn off very rapidly if I'd agreed to do what she wanted,' he said, with a shrug. 'A genuine migraine can be hellish, I'm told, but Elizabeth only had them when she was thwarted.'

He slid his hands down to her neck, caressing her nape with the tips of his fingers and stroking her gently behind the ears with his thumbs.

'If you and I had met a month later, it's very probable—in fact it's a certainty—that I'd have been on my own again. We were coming to the end of the road, Elizabeth and I. That's the truth, Maggie. Don't you trust me?'

'Yes...yes, of course I do.' She turned her head to press a kiss on his wrist. 'It's just that...loving you myself...I can't quite believe that anyone could live with you and *not* love you.'

'I find it equally hard to believe that you can have reached the ripe age of twenty-five without being snapped up,' he told her. 'How could it happen, I ask myself, that this lovely, intelligent, sexy, successful woman is still free? Although not for much longer.'

As he bent towards her, Maggie closed her eyes, the better to feel the first soft brush of his lips on hers.

She had been kissed a good deal during her student days, but not very often recently, and never the way Adam kissed her, gently pressing her backwards against the feather-filled cushions with which the sofa was heaped until she was lying relaxed with her arms round his neck and he was leaning over her.

As one long kiss merged with another, she felt she was drowning in bliss. The slight roughness of his skin only intensified her pleasure. It was part of the exciting contrast between his tall, powerful body and her smaller, softer one.

It seemed that he was experiencing the same pleasure in reverse. Presently he murmured huskily, 'You're so soft and silky...your hair...your skin...'

A moment later she was surprised to discover that, without her being aware of it, he had unfastened her shirt.

'I remember wanting to do this on the beach that first day,' he said, as his hand slid behind her, searching for the clip of her bra.

'Oh, Adam...oh, darling...' She gave a small moan of pleasure as he disposed of the flimsy barrier between his palm and her flesh, sending shivers of delight along her nerves as his fingers explored her breasts.

His lips were discovering the sensitive places behind her ears and under her chin. Wherever he touched her, with warm lips and caressing hands, her skin seemed to grow a hundred new nerve-ends, all of them flickering with pleasure and sending ecstatic messages to the core of her being.

Even when he slid an arm under her knees and rose from the sofa with her cradled in his arms, it didn't break the spell. Wherever he was taking her was where she wanted to go.

Moonlight was streaming through the window of his room at the top of the house, but the bed was in the shadow of the sloping ceiling.

Adam lowered her on to it, then straightened and began to undress. For the first time she saw the full splendour of his tall, powerful body as he rapidly shed his clothes, all the time gazing down at her with eyes which burned like blue steel in the silver light. Naked, he was all taut flesh and rippling muscle as he put one knee on the bed and swooped down to kiss her.

Delightedly she slid her hands over his warm, sleek skin, a sensation as satisfying as stroking polished wood or sculpted bronze.

'I've been dreaming of this all my life...' he murmured in her ear. 'Oh, Maggie...my lovely girl...'

Carefully, gently, as if he were unwrapping a very precious object, he finished undressing her.

Aware that he wanted her now, this instant, and was forcing himself to go slowly for her sake, she whispered, 'I've dreamt of it, too. Every night...since you first kissed me.'

After which she lost the power to speak and could only give gasps and smothered cries as Adam showed her how far her imagination had fallen short of the reality of his passion.

Time, she discovered, stopped when she was in his arms. She had no idea whether it was half an hour or two hours later that he put an end to her delicious languor by saying quietly, 'I should like to keep you here all night, but you may feel you should go back to the hotel.'

Maggie, who had been enjoying a state of mental and physical well-being superior to anything she had experienced in her entire life, had no wish to bestir herself. But after a moment or two the implications of his remark penetrated her happy daze and made her sit up.

'What time is it?'

'Not late. The hotel won't be locked up for some time yet.' He trailed his fingers down her spine. 'We have time to open some champagne and discuss where to go for our honeymoon, which is going to start almost immediately if I have my way.'

'I thought it had started already—unofficially,' said Maggie, laughing, as she swung herself off the bed and began to retrieve her clothes. 'I would much rather spend the night here, but it would be sure to cause talk, and on a small island like this I expect gossip spreads like wildfire. I don't want all the old ladies clicking their tongues and disapproving of me. As for our honeymoon . . . I'll happily leave that to you.' In her bra and panties, she paused to say seriously, 'If you go on as you've begun, it's going to be heavenly anywhere.'

Adam, now also dressing, laughed and bowed from the waist. 'Them's my sentiments, too.' He caught her to him. 'You kept me at arm's length for a long time, Miss Hornchurch, but when I finally got close it was all and more than I'd hoped for.' He kissed her. 'To hell with all the old ladies . . . why should we sleep apart when we could be together?'

Maggie would have agreed, but just then the telephone rang. Reluctantly letting her go, he moved away to answer it.

'Hello?'

'Adam, I must talk to——'

The voice was a woman's. Her tone was high-pitched, distraught.

'Not now. I'm busy. I'll call you back tomorrow.' Adam's interruption was cold, curt and dismissive. He didn't bang down the receiver, but the way he replaced it indicated irritation. 'That reminds me, I switched off the answering machine without checking the messages. I'd better do that,' he said. 'And I'll also contact my business manager and tell him he'll have to reshuffle my schedule. Luckily I haven't any unbreakable engagements in the next two weeks. How about you?'

'I don't think so.'

Who was that woman? she wanted to ask, but didn't, hoping he would tell her without being asked.

But when Adam had finished dressing he said, 'I'll go down and open the champagne,' and left the room without making any reference to the frantic-sounding appeal which he had dealt with so tersely.

Perhaps he doesn't realise I heard what she said, thought Maggie, sitting down to put on her tights.

Her bag being downstairs, she used the horn comb with which he had just tidied his rumpled black hair. Beside it, on top of the chest of drawers which, with a mirror on the wall behind it, served as his dressing-table, lay a pair of silver-monogrammed ivory-backed men's hairbrushes. The entwined initials were R.R., not A.R. Probably the brushes had belonged to Adam's father or grandfather.

One day they would pass to his son, who would also be her son.

But the thought of the happy years which now lay ahead, the nights of love and days of satisfying companionship when the demands of their careers allowed them time to be together, did not fill her with quite the same unalloyed joy as it would have done a short while ago—before that disturbing telephone call.

When she went downstairs she found Adam in the sitting-room, filling two tall, tulip-shaped glasses with champagne.

'How does a honeymoon on one of the western isles of Scotland appeal to you?' he asked. 'It's beautiful there when the weather's good and, if there are some wet days, we can find ways to amuse ourselves.'

'It sounds fine to me.' Maggie took the glass he handed to her and returned his smile.

The identity of the woman on the telephone was still worrying her. At the same time she didn't want to spoil this memorable moment in their lives by bringing up something which Adam preferred to ignore.

'To us,' he said, taking her left hand in his and raising his glass with his other.

'To us,' she echoed, before sipping the wine.

'What sort of ring would you like?' he asked, lifting her hand to look at the inexpensive but pretty moonstone set in silver ring she was wearing on her little finger. 'My mother left me some antique rings, as did my grandmother. They're in my bank here. We can look at them tomorrow, or you may prefer to design yourself a ring.'

Discussing this and how to avoid having their wedding turned into a circus by the Press, they drank two glasses of champagne each. Then Adam escorted her across the road, having first kissed her goodnight in the privacy of the outer hall of his house.

Later, lying awake, Maggie's thoughts were not of engagement rings and wedding dresses—for even a quiet wedding called for something special to wear—but of those five agitated words spoken, she felt sure, by Elizabeth Vazon.

Surely, however much it might have embarrassed him to be rung up by his former mistress soon after making love to his future wife, Adam would not have reacted as he had unless calls from Elizabeth were a frequent occurrence? Which suggested that whatever he might say about her not being upset by the ending of their relationship, she *was* upset . . . very upset.

Maggie didn't like the feeling that her happiness, when it was made public, would cause someone else great pain. Nor was she comfortable with the idea that Adam had assured her Elizabeth wasn't heartbroken when he knew that she was.

She was woken by the telephone.

'Hello?'

'Good morning. I hope I haven't dragged you out of the bath,' said Adam's voice.

'You've just woken me up.' She looked at her watch. 'Oh, goodness, I've overslept. It's gone half-past nine.'

'I was expecting you to join me for breakfast, but don't hurry yourself. We'll make it brunch instead. Meanwhile I'll go to the bank and get out the family jewels for you to look at. See you later, darling.' He made a kissing sound and rang off.

As she'd been awake half the night, it wasn't surprising that without an alarm to rouse her she was still in bed. She had finished dressing and, from force of habit while her mind was preoccupied, had just made the bed when the telephone rang again.

'There's a lady downstairs to see you, Miss Hornchurch.'

Maggie recognised the voice of the receptionist.

'A lady? Who is she?'

'Mrs Vazon. Shall I send her up?'

Elizabeth Vazon . . . here . . . to see her? Maggie's mind boggled.

After a pause, she said, 'Yes, would you send her up, please?'

As she replaced the receiver, automatically she glanced round the room to see if any tidying was needed before her visitor arrived. What could Elizabeth Vazon possibly want with her? How did she even know who Maggie was or that she was staying here?

There was a tap at the door. Maggie went to open it.

In the corridor stood the girl in the photograph Mrs Perelle had shown her the day she arrived in Guernsey. Now in her late twenties, Elizabeth was even more lovely than she had been in the first flush of her beauty. She was probably six or seven pounds thinner than when the photograph was taken, and the exquisite structure of her oval face was more clearly defined.

In the intervening years she had acquired a polish and elegance which the girl in the photograph had lacked. At the moment she looked as if she had stepped from the pages of *Vogue*. She was wearing a suit of fine gabardine, the colour of Guernsey cream, with a matching silk shirt. Her ear-rings, bracelets and beads were made of new ivory, indicating that she wasn't a person who worried about where her adornments came from. No longer shoulder-length and casual as it had been in the wedding photograph, her fair hair was now styled in the latest fashion, and subtle, expert make-up emphasised eyes and lips which clearly were strikingly lovely without any artificial aid.

She was the kind of woman who made other women acutely conscious of their own defects. Maggie knew she couldn't hold a candle to this gorgeous creature smiling uncertainly at her.

'Won't you come in?' she invited, holding the door open.

'It's good of you to see a total stranger, Miss Hornchurch. You must be wondering what I want,' said the other girl, entering the bedroom and glancing around it with a look of faint surprise. 'How very tidy you are. If it weren't for your books'—with a gesture at the night table—'one wouldn't know this room was occupied.'

'There's a cabinet in the bathroom for my cosmetics. It makes life easier for the maids if one doesn't leave too many things about. Won't you sit down?' Maggie indicated the armchair and seated herself on the side of the bed. 'You're not a total stranger, Mrs Vazon. Mrs Perelle showed me a photograph of you and your husband and Adam on the day I arrived. But I'm puzzled that you know who I am.'

'Not many of the vineries are still growing grapes these days, but the other kind of grapevine is flourishing,' said her visitor. 'News travels fast on this island. Everyone knows what everyone else is up to. But actually I heard about you a long time ago...when Adam and I were on holiday together in Barbados. It was I who suggested you as a possible designer for the house in Spain. There was an article about you in the magazine I was reading on our flight there. I showed it to Adam. He would never have heard of you if it hadn't been for me.'

She paused and gave a deep sigh. 'And a great deal of trouble and unhappiness would have been avoided.' Her gaze drifted round the room and then she fixed her large grey-green luminous eyes on Maggie's face. 'Perhaps you are not aware that, until you came on the scene, Adam and I were very close friends...very close.'

'Certainly I'm aware of it, Mrs Vazon. Adam has talked about your relationship. According to him, it was never intended to be permanent. You were both marking time, as it were, until either or both of you met the person you were really waiting for.'

'I wasn't waiting for anyone. I fell in love with Adam when I was fourteen years old. *My* feelings have never changed. I married another man, yes. And bitterly regretted it. But I never stopped loving Adam. I never shall...and one day I know he'll come back to me. We belong together. We always have. We're like Cathy and Heathcliff in *Wuthering Heights*. No matter what mad thing either of us does, however much we hurt each other, he and I were born to love each other.'

As she spoke, her great eyes filled with tears which brimmed over and ran down her cheeks, making her fumble in her bag for a handkerchief.

She sniffed. 'I'm so sorry... I didn't mean to be emotional. I realise that, if you love Adam, you're going to be badly hurt too. But better that than to find yourself married to a man whose heart belongs to another woman. Believe me, I speak from experience. I married, loving someone else, and it was a disaster from day one.'

For some moments Maggie was nonplussed. As her mind grappled with the situation, the first conclusion to emerge was that this beautiful, sophisticated woman wouldn't have come to see her, wouldn't have poured out her heart in this moving way, unless there was some force in her claim that she and Adam belonged together.

Equally, Maggie couldn't believe that Adam had lied or even misled her about ending his affair with Elizabeth. But was he misleading himself? Was there an imperishable bond between him and this glamorous creature whom he had known all his life?

'May I have a glass of water, please?' Elizabeth asked huskily.

'Of course.' Maggie jumped up and went to the adjoining bathroom, where she washed out the tumbler holding her toothbrush and filled it with some of the bottled spring water she always drank last thing at night. Possibly the island's water was better than London's bad-tasting tap water, but she preferred to drink spring water.

As Elizabeth took the glass from her, Maggie noticed the other girl's slender hands and perfectly manicured nails. Her organisation of her own life included cutting out things which were time-consuming and impracticable. Long coloured nails were one of them. She kept her nails short and painted them with clear varnish, which didn't show chips, twice a week.

'There's something else which you probably haven't considered,' Elizabeth said, after sipping some water. 'You're English...an incomer. Guernsey people are very clannish, even now...perhaps even more so now that so many people have come to live here.'

'Guernsey people strike me as exceptionally friendly and nice,' said Maggie. 'The other day in a shop, when they didn't have what I wanted, they directed me to another shop. That isn't usual on the mainland.'

'Oh, yes, we're friendly to visitors. Tourism is part of the island's economy. But that doesn't mean there is much social intermingling between islanders and incomers,' said the other girl. 'There is some, but not very much. You would always be made aware that you didn't really *belong* here in the way that Adam and I do.'

'Mrs Perelle is English by birth. She's said nothing to me to suggest that she doesn't feel she belongs here.'

'I think her husband married her during the war when he was in the Forces. Quite a lot of Guernsey men married mainland girls then. They had no option. I expect it worked out in some cases. It doesn't usually. The fact that we speak English here now, and you rarely hear the *patois* except when the older country people are talking among themselves, doesn't alter the fact that we *aren't* English. Marriage is never an easy relationship. A mixed marriage is doubly difficult.

'And there's another thing...' said Elizabeth. 'You're a career woman, aren't you? Adam needs a full-time wife. His life is very stressful. He needs someone who is free to tour with him, to be there whenever he needs

her. Not someone involved in a separate and often conflicting career. How much does your work mean to you?'

'It means a great deal. I love it. It's my living and my
greatest pleasure ... as important to me as his music is
to Adam. Have you never worked, Mrs Vazon?'

'Do call me Elizabeth. No, I've never worked for my
living. My father was a rich man. He thought it would
be wrong for me to take a job which some other girl
really needed. But I haven't lived a life of idleness. I've
taken various courses in London ... art appreci-
ation ... cookery. I've also studied languages. I'm fluent
in French and German and quite good at Spanish. I've
trained myself to be the kind of wife Adam needs. Ask
yourself, Maggie—are you?'

'I think so, yes,' Maggie answered. But suddenly all
her certainties were blowing hither and thither like
autumn leaves in a gale.

The one thing she was sure of, in all this mental con-
fusion, was that the girl sitting opposite her matched
Adam in looks and style far better than she ever could.
Elizabeth wasn't only beautiful and expensively dressed
and groomed, she had the same innate star quality as he
did, only hers was dormant, undeveloped. Perhaps if
her father's wealth hadn't made it unnecessary for her
to work, she might have become an actress or a model
or TV presenter.

'Adam would be furious with me if he knew I'd come
to see you. Please don't tell him, will you? I don't want
him to know I would go to these lengths for him. I have
no pride where he's concerned. I've already lost the good
opinion of many people here by being involved with him.
The first time we went away together it was mentioned
in the tabloid gossip columns. It isn't possible to have

a discreet relationship with someone as much in the public eye as he is.'

Maggie said, 'One of my staff—a great fan of his—told me he was one of the few people in show business who managed to keep his private life totally private. Anyway, so many people live together on a committed basis nowadays that it's hardly a matter for disapproval any more.'

'Not on the mainland, no. But Guernsey is more old-fashioned. Here some people do disapprove of irregular relationships, and I'm persona non grata with them and shall be...until Adam comes back to me. Then I'll be forgiven.' Elizabeth rose. 'I mustn't keep you any longer. Thank you for seeing me. I'm sorry I had to come and upset you but, as I said earlier, better now than later.'

With her hand on the doorknob she turned, saying regretfully, 'I think we could have been great friends if we hadn't been in love with the same man. If I were you, I should go back to London and get on with the career which you're making such a success of. There'll be someone else whose life will mesh with yours much better than Adam's ever could.'

'Are you sure you aren't allowing your feelings for him to cloud your judgement about his feelings for you?' Maggie asked quietly.

Elizabeth shook her head. "I know Adam very well...perhaps better than he does himself. Don't be deceived by his easy-going charm. That's superficial. Underneath it, he's a complex man. I hurt him once, very badly, and I think, perhaps subconsciously, he needs to hurt me in return. I'm afraid you're caught up in a situation which may have no solution. All I know is that Adam and I have been through too much together for him ever to get me out of his system completely...or I

him. If you're prepared to accept him on those terms...'
She gave a slight shrug. 'I must go now. Goodbye.'

She opened the door and a moment later was gone,
leaving Maggie not knowing what to think.

Less than an hour later she was airborne over the
Channel, recalled to London by a telephone call from
the studio. Alice had slipped on the stairs and broken
her right wrist.

The flight gave Maggie an hour in which to think about
what she should say to Adam when she rang him from
London. She had scribbled a hasty message to him, explaining what had happened and promising to call him
later in the day. The hotel receptionist, who had been
most helpful in ringing the airport and organising a taxi
while Maggie packed her belongings, had promised to
take the note across the road for her.

Whether Adam had returned from the shopping centre
of St Peter Port in time to jump into his car and follow
her to the airport was something she wouldn't find out
until she spoke to him. If he had, this time he had been
too late to catch her before she took off. For that she
was deeply thankful. She wasn't ready to discuss the
situation with him yet.

The short flight back to the mainland was one of the
unhappiest hours of her life; far worse than the sleepless
night she had spent returning from Barbados.

She had been uneasy in her mind ever since Adam had
put the receiver down on Elizabeth the night before; and
now that she had met the other woman, and liked her,
she was convinced that Adam's past wasn't as over and
done with as he wanted her to believe.

On landing she called the studio and was told that
Alice was still at the hospital where her wrist was being

set. Ted Drayton had driven her there and was still with her, so she was in good hands. Even so, Maggie felt that seeing Alice was her first priority.

For a girl with a badly broken wrist, Alice was looking surprisingly pleased with life as she greeted Maggie with an apology for causing her to rush back.

Then, responding to Maggie's enquiries about the accident with a casual, 'I lost my balance and fell awkwardly,' she went on to tell her big news, which was that she and Ted were going to be married. 'As soon as my wrist is out of plaster, but don't worry—I shan't give up working.'

'That's wonderful news. Congratulations, Ted. I'm delighted for you both,' Maggie said warmly, hiding the pain she felt because about twelve hours ago she been aglow like Alice.

She returned to the studio, expecting to find that Adam had telephoned. He hadn't, which was rather surprising. Perhaps he had decided to follow her to London.

Having dealt with one or two urgent matters which Alice would normally have handled, Maggie rang Guernsey.

Adam answered the telephone. When she had told him that Alice expected to be back at work the next day, although considerably incommoded by her injured wrist, he said, 'Are you coming back tonight or shall I come over to London?'

'No, I shan't come back tonight. I shall have to work late. Various things have cropped up which need my attention. I couldn't see you tonight if you did come over.'

'I shouldn't have thought anything was more important than the plans we began to make last night. Surely you can spare me an hour this evening? You have to eat. Why can't we have dinner together?' There was a definite edge of sarcasm in his voice.

'It's a long way to come to have a quick bite together. I feel our plans can wait a few days until this slight crisis at the studio is over.' When he made no comment, she went on, 'Last night we were both rather carried away. If I hadn't been called back here I was going to talk to you this morning about... about whether it's really the best plan to get married immediately. Perhaps we should see how our working lives mesh. The majority of people do have a trial run first now. It really makes a lot of sense.'

'Not to me, it doesn't,' said Adam. 'Nor did it to you—last night.'

'As I said, last night was an emotional "high", which isn't the ideal state of mind for making very serious decisions.'

'Is there something behind all this which you're not telling me, Maggie?'

There was, but she had promised Elizabeth not to mention her visit, and, as Adam himself had chosen to ignore Elizabeth's call to him the night before, she answered, 'I expect having parents who changed partners more than once makes me preternaturally cautious.'

'Don't lie to me, Maggie,' he said sharply. 'Not even by default. I'm pretty sure this sudden change of attitude is the result of Elizabeth's visit to the hotel this morning. Mrs Perelle caught sight of her driving her car round to the car park at the back of the building. Later I checked out what she was doing there. She was calling on you.'

'Yes, she was,' Maggie admitted. 'But even before she came to see me I wasn't happy about the way you dealt with her telephone call last night. It wasn't a nice way to treat someone with whom, by your own admission, you've been very closely involved. And was it being truthful to tell me that Elizabeth didn't care about breaking up with you? No, it damn well wasn't. She does care—deeply.'

There was a silence at the other end of the line. Then he said, in an angry tone, 'We can't possibly discuss this on the telephone. I'm coming over. My own plane is out of commission, but I'll come over by Channel Airways. I doubt if any of the urgent matters on your desk are so urgent they won't keep until we've sorted out our problems. I'll be there as soon as possible.'

Without even saying goodbye, he ended the call.

Less than half an hour later he rang back to say that his chances of getting off the island that day were not good. A flight had had to be cancelled for technical reasons, which meant that all unsold seats on the rest of the day's flights were now full.

'Which means you will have to come here. I've already booked you on the last flight of the day. I'll be at the airport to meet you.'

'I'm sorry, you'll have to unbook me. I didn't get much sleep last night and I don't feel like trekking all the way back to the airport,' Maggie replied. 'Anyway, I think a few days of calm reflection are called for, Adam.'

She heard an exasperated exclamation. With audibly strained patience, he said, 'You don't have to "fly the Tube" to the airport, for goodness' sake. Order a car. Hang on...I'll give you the number of the firm I use. Better still, I'll lay it on for you. You don't have to lift a finger.'

Maggie had spent the intervening twenty minutes dealing with an overdue special order for very expensive fittings and not getting satisfactory answers about why they were late, or when they could be expected. Tired and stressed, she knew she was in no state to handle this fraught situation which had sprung, like some horrible fungus, out of the warm summer grass of last night's ecstatic happiness.

'Thank you, but no,' she said firmly. 'It's still an hour's drive—perhaps more—through rush-hour traffic. That's not on—not tonight. Why don't you come over tomorrow and we'll have lunch?'

'I don't believe this!' Adam sounded aghast. 'This isn't a business deal we're discussing. This is us... our marriage... our future. Last night you told me you loved me.'

'I know...and I meant it. But you haven't been straight with me, Adam. And besides that, there's the problem of fitting our careers together. The fact that, in spite of Alice's accident, you expect me to come running back there is proof of the problems that face us. Elizabeth told me that you needed a full-time wife, not someone with a separate career.'

There was a muttered expletive which she didn't catch before he said coldly, 'Possibly I'm the best judge of the kind of wife I need. Very well...I'll see you tomorrow.'

He then made some polite enquiries about Alice's wrist and rang off, leaving Maggie wishing that the walls of her office were not made of glass which prevented her from putting her head on her arms and having a much-needed weep.

Next morning a special messenger delivered a letter to her. It was from Adam. 'Dear Maggie', he had written— the letter bore today's date and must have been written during the night or very early this morning.

If there is one thing above all others that I require in my wife, it is trust. Clearly you do not trust me and perhaps never will. This is particularly unfortunate because my wife's faith in me will be put to the test more often and more severely than that of most wives.

There will be times when I shall be away from home, perhaps for extended periods. Sometimes my name will be linked with other women by the papers and periodicals which specialise in such innuendoes. A jealous woman, or one who doubts my integrity, will make both our lives unbearable.

For you to take someone else's word against mine, *before* we are married, is not a good augury.

In the circumstances, I have decided not to go ahead with the house at Pobla de Cabres and shall ask Oliver Thornham to re-sell it for me.

I'm sorry it has to end like this, but if life has taught me anything it's that in these situations the clean cut is less painful than a slow break-up.

I wish you well. Adam.

CHAPTER SIX

THE week following the delivery of Adam's letter was the worst week of Maggie's life. She plumbed depths of pain and hopelessness which made the traumas of her childhood seem trivial by comparison. Against this crushing blow her spirit had no resilience. But in public she kept up a bright front, and none of her colleagues guessed her real state of mind.

In the evenings she tried to work, but found it harder to concentrate than during the day when the presence of other people forced her to keep her mind on what she was doing.

Every night, alone in her flat, she read and re-read the cold, formal words with which Adam had expressed his decision to end their troubled and ultimately disastrous love-affair.

Many times she began letters to him. Many times she picked up the telephone and began to dial the code for Guernsey, only to change her mind before completing his number.

Throughout that first endless week, she lived in hope that he would regret his letter and telephone her. But although the telephone did ring, making her heart beat wildly and her fingers shake as she snatched up the receiver, it was never his voice which answered her tense, 'Hello?'

The worst times were after she had gone to bed. Unable to sleep, her mind going over and over the manner of their parting and the insoluble question of who was to blame, she would find herself remembering Adam's kisses and caresses and her own abandoned response to them.

She didn't know whether to regret what had happened in the moonlit room at the top of the old house, or to be thankful that just once in her life she had experienced those soaring peaks of emotion. They would never happen again. She was sure of that.

Setting out for Bath with William, Maggie was determined to be a cheerful companion on the journey and to enjoy the weekend with his family, whom she was genuinely looking forward to meeting.

William was in high spirits. During the week he had signed an important contract to make staff-training videos for the British section of an international company, a contract he had won in the face of strong competition.

For the first hour of the journey they talked about this, and about the commission which Maggie felt had put her business on its feet.

'The great thing about you is that your eyes don't glaze when I mention things like overheads,' William said, glancing at her. 'You have to worry about them yourself, so they're not a subject which bores you.'

'Not a bit...it's good to have someone to compare notes with,' she answered, smiling at him.

He took a hand off the wheel and patted her knee. 'It's going to be a great weekend,' he said happily.

She could tell he was looking forward to breaking his good news to his family.

His parents' house was in a tall Georgian terrace of substantial double-fronted houses near the centre of Bath Spa. Although it had no front garden, there was one at the rear with a building which had once housed a horse and carriage and was now a large garage.

Having tucked his car alongside the two already there, William hoisted his grip and Maggie's weekend case from the boot and they walked up the long garden, to be greeted first by his sister Jane, who was playing with her two small children. They were happy to be hugged by their uncle but were shy of Maggie.

'Make the most of it,' said their mother, laughing. 'Once they've got used to you, they'll be *too* friendly. Mum's in the kitchen, William. She's supposed to be leading the life of a lady of leisure this weekend, but she insisted on making a treacle tart for your lunch.'

The kitchen was in the basement, which they reached by descending steps from the lawn to a paved area where Jane's husband Dick and the boyfriend of another sister were drinking beer in the sun.

'I'll take your luggage upstairs while you're saying hello to Laura,' said Dick, relieving his brother-in-law of the bags.

Laura Bramshott was just the sort of mother Maggie had longed for when she was a child. A plump woman in her fifties, with traces of youthful prettiness still to be seen in her kind unmade-up face, she gave a cry of pleasure at the sight of her son.

'William, dear... how are you?' She hugged him to her generous bosom before turning her blue eyes on the girl who was with him. 'And this is Maggie. I'm delighted to meet you, my dear. I'm afraid you're going to think this house a terrible hotchpotch and not very tidy, to boot, but at least all the beds are comfortable and there's plenty of hot water for showers, which is the main thing, isn't it?'

'The vital thing,' Maggie agreed. 'It's very kind of you to have me, Mrs Bramshott.'

'Call me Laura, dear. Everyone does. William, show Maggie where she's going to sleep and where the bathroom is. She'll want to freshen up before lunch. I've made your favourite pud,' she added, beaming fondly at him.

'Treacle tart? Marvellous. You haven't lived till you've tried Mum's treacle tart,' he said.

'Maggie won't want to spoil her nice slim figure. There's fruit salad for the girls. I remember how it used to annoy me, having to be polite and eat John's mother's fattening food when we were engaged,' said Mrs Bramshott. 'I've always had a problem keeping my weight down ... even when I was your age,' she confided to Maggie. 'My husband and sons are just the opposite. They eat like horses and never put on an ounce.'

'We don't sit about reading novels as much as you do,' said a tall, grey-haired man, entering the kitchen in time to hear this remark.

Mrs Bramshott gave a hoot of laughter. 'Fat chance of that in this household. This is my husband, Maggie.'

'How do you do, Dr Bramshott.'

Maggie held out her hand and received a firm clasp and a smile from William's father before he turned to his son and gave him a one-armed hug, saying affectionately, 'Hello, old boy. How are things going?'

'They're really beginning to take off, Dad. I've got a lot to tell you. I'm just going to take Maggie upstairs. I'll be right back.'

As William shepherded her out of the kitchen, Maggie was sharply aware of the close and loving relationship between him and his parents and between the doctor and his wife.

On the way up three flights of stairs she could see what Mrs Bramshott had meant by describing her home as a hotchpotch. No carefully thought out plan had governed the decoration and furnishing of this house. Each flight had a different carpet, different curtains at the landing windows and different wallpaper. Maggie guessed they had been chosen because they were of good quality but reduced in price. With a family of five to raise, Mrs Bramshott wouldn't have had the money to redecorate at one fell swoop, and probably she was a woman who felt that it didn't matter too much if curtains and carpets didn't 'go', as long as they would wear well. At least, that was Maggie's impression as she followed William up to a bedroom with two single beds, one with a new-looking duvet on it and the other with an old-fashioned eiderdown over a candlewick bedspread.

'It looks as if Joey and Susie haven't arrived yet,' said William. 'They're supposed to be here for lunch, but maybe Joey's old banger has broken down on the way. Goodness knows how it ever got through its last MOT test.' He opened a freestanding wardrobe. 'Oh, good…someone's made room for you and Susie to hang things. As you see, there's a hand basin in here and the bathroom's across the landing with another, separate loo next door to it. I hope you're going to be comfortable. It's not what you're used to, I'm afraid.'

She smiled at him. 'You have no idea how lucky you are to have grown up in a house like this with parents who adore each other and you. I'd have given the earth to be part of a family like yours, William.'

He put his hands on her shoulders. 'I'm hoping to persuade you to become part of this family.'

Before she had fully taken it in, he leaned forward and kissed her very gently on the lips.

'Don't say anything now,' he told her. 'Just think about it, will you? I now you don't feel about me the way I feel about you...yet. But maybe you could if you put your mind to it, Maggie darling. We'll talk about it later...OK?'

After giving her shoulders a squeeze, he dropped his hands and left her.

Maggie's case was lying open on the bed with the eiderdown, and she had almost finished her unpacking when she heard someone running up the stairs. Moments later there was a tap on the half-open door and a girl in her late teens came in.

'Hello, I'm Susie...Joey's girl.' She was wearing a bright red sweatshirt with *J'aime le Ski* printed across the chest. Her dark hair was caught up by two red plastic butterfly-clips.

'I'm Maggie...a friend of William's. You've stayed here before, I expect?'

'Lots of times. Joey and I met on a school skiing trip. We're unofficially engaged. Our parents all say we have to wait until we're older to make it official, but as far as we're concerned it is now. We're nineteen,' Susie added.

'It does seem a little young to decide on something as important as your partner for life,' said Maggie.

Susie hoisted a roll-bag on to the other bed and unzipped it. 'We're mature for our age, and we've known each other for four years, which is a lot longer than most people know each other before committing themselves. What are you wearing tonight? I'm wearing this.' She delved in the bag and brought out a bundle of red silk which, vigorously shaken, revealed itself as a somewhat crumpled disco dress with puffy sleeves, a low neck and a flounced mini-skirt. 'I'll have to press it after lunch.'

'Yes, mine could do with a press, too.' Maggie took her dress from the wardrobe.

It was made of her favourite after-dark fabric, black chiffon, and was very plain, even severe, except that the skirt had a slit which didn't show when she stood still but as soon as she moved revealed almost as much of her left leg as Susie's skirt would show of both legs.

Susie, not noticing the slit, made polite noises about it but clearly thought it rather dull. Which, like a lot of great dresses, it was—on a hanger.

Some hours later, when she saw it on Maggie, she revised her opinion, saying admiringly, 'You look fabulous. That's how I'd like to look, but with my round face and snub nose I'm never going to look sophisticated.'

Maggie thought she looked sweet with clusters of glass beads like bunches of ripe red currants dangling from her ears, and red tights and low-heeled red pumps.

She wasn't sure that her own appearance might not be a shade too sophisticated for an informal dance at a country hotel. They were all going by taxi so that the men of the party didn't have to limit their alcohol intake.

William and Joey were both in the large ground-floor sitting-room when Maggie and Susie went downstairs. William was wearing a dinner-jacket, his younger brother a lounge suit.

'Hi, guys. How do we look?' Susie bounced into the room with one hand on her hip and the other behind her head.

She was full of fun and animation and Joey was equally exuberant. Observing them during lunch, Maggie had come to the conclusion that they were so much alike, so in tune with each other temperamentally, that in spite of their youth their love for each other would last.

'Don't stand still with your mouth open, or someone may post a letter in it. No, no ... I take it all back ... you look great,' Joey grinned, dodging the punch Susie aimed at him.

There was a rock record playing and the two young things began to dance.

William said nothing, but his expression told Maggie that he liked everything about her: the dress, the big rhinestone star pinned on her shoulder, the two smaller stars in her ears, the sheer black tights, the high-heeled shoes.

They had had no more private conversation since he had left her upstairs on her own before lunch. During lunch they hadn't sat next to each other, but on opposite sides of the long dining-table originally made to accommodate a large Victorian family and serving that purpose again with the Bramshotts and their children and children's friends.

Several times during the meal Maggie had felt William watching her, but had avoided returning his gaze.

She couldn't pretend that his declaration in the bedroom had come as a complete surprise. She had sensed for some time that he might be growing serious about her, although she hadn't been certain. How could a woman ever be certain until a man stated his feelings?

But now, as he looked at her with the unmistakable ardour of a man gazing at a woman he finds desirable, she knew she must make the decision to let their friendship progress into courtship, or to make it clear that she couldn't ever reciprocate his feelings towards her.

'You look beautiful, Maggie,' he said, holding both hands out so that she had little option but to give him her hands.

'You look very debonair yourself. You're amazingly like your father. I thought sons usually took after their mothers,' she said lightly, tightening her fingers for a second or two before quickly withdrawing them. 'Joey is like her, of course.' Deliberately she turned away to watch the others gyrating in time to the beat.

'What would you like to drink?' he asked.

Maggie looked at the array of bottles on the side table he indicated.

'A Campari and soda, please... not too much Campari.'

While William fixed her drink, she looked at the room in more detail, noting its handsome proportions and guessing that when the house was new it would have been an elegant drawing-room.

'Here you are.' William's fingers brushed hers as he handed her a tall glass with ice and a twist of lemon floating close to the surface of the cerise-tinted soda.

'Thank you.' She knew she ought not to let her thoughts wander to other things when the problem of how to deal with his implied proposal of marriage was still unresolved in her mind.

'Let's go somewhere quieter.' He took her free hand in his. She had left her coat and bag on a chair in the hall.

Across the hall was a small room furnished like a study.

'This used to be Dad's consulting-room before he went into group practice and they had a surgery built. Now it's used by anyone who needs peace and quiet,' he explained, closing the door. 'Look, I know better than to make love to a girl who's just done her face. One advantage of having three sisters is that you pick up a lot of inside information about the opposite sex. But I must have five minutes alone with you before the festivities start.' Recapturing her hand, he drew her closer. 'Have you thought about what I said to you before lunch? Did you understand what I was getting at?'

'I think so...you were suggesting that we might get married, weren't you?'

He nodded. 'How does it strike you?'

Before she could answer, he went on, 'You've never mentioned anyone, but I've always had the feeling that, like me, you'd fallen in love with the wrong person when you were younger and didn't want to go through all that pain again. Am I right?'

'I didn't realise you'd had an unhappy love-affair, William,' she said, startled.

'It was a long time ago. I'm over it now...completely. I felt pretty low at the time, but what happened was for the best. I see that now.'

'Who was she? What went wrong?'

'She was the sister of a friend at college. They were Indians. His name was Salman and hers was Mona. They were both very good-looking. Their mother had been a film star before she married. The whole family was spending some years in England because of the father's job, and they seemed just like us...on the surface. Mona's mother wore a sari and they ate Indian food at home, but otherwise they seemed more cosmopolitan and sophisticated than my parents. That made it more of a shock when I found out that Mona was going to be married to the son of some friends of her father. It had been arranged when they were children, and she accepted the arrangement. She loved me, or said she did, but not enough to go against her parents' wishes. She felt they must know what was best for her.'

'Oh, William...poor you. I had no idea.'

'The thing is that they were right...her parents, I mean. It wouldn't have worked...she and I. There were lots of cultural differences under the surface, and she wouldn't have liked living in England for good. It's better to marry someone with whom you have most things in common. That's why my parents have been happy together. They're almost the same age, they have very similar backgrounds and they wanted the same things out of life. As I feel you and I do. Don't you feel that? That we're two of a kind?'

'Yes...in many ways I think we are,' Maggie agreed cautiously. 'But I also feel people should be very sure of their feelings before they marry, and I'm not sure I'm ready for such a serious commitment yet.'

He said, 'You haven't told me if I was right in thinking you'd also had an unhappy experience?'

'Yes, you were,' she admitted. But what he didn't realise, and she was reluctant to tell him, was how recently hers had occurred.

'Can you talk about it?' he asked, obviously curious.

'I...I fell for someone who, in a different way, was as unsuitable for me as Mona was for you. Our lifestyles were totally different...and there were other complications.'

'Poor you,' William said gently, echoing her exclamation of sympathy. He put down his glass and took hers and set it beside his. Then, taking her hands in his, he said, 'I've suspected all along there was something like that in the background...something preventing our friendship from developing, on your side, as fast as it has on mine. I love you very much, Maggie. I know we can be happy together...and you needn't worry that I'd expect you to settle down and be a *hausfrau* like Mum. I know how much your work means to you. Being married shouldn't mean that people stop having lives of their own and personal ambitions. I would never interfere with your career or resent the time you gave to it. We'd both help and support each other.'

Maggie couldn't help returning the pressure of his fingers. 'Oh, William, you're such a nice, kind, understanding man, I ought to be falling over myself to marry you,' she said, full of warm feelings towards him—but not feelings which added up to the passionate love he deserved.

'But you're not,' he said, with a wry smile. 'For a while, on the way down this morning, I felt there was a chance I might be able to announce our engagement at the party tonight. My parents took to you on sight. Not that it would have mattered to me if they hadn't, but it's nice that they're equally keen to have you join the clan. Never mind—if you don't feel you can say yes yet, I won't pressure you. Although I plan to try some gentle persuasion later on, when it doesn't matter about smudging your lipstick.'

He took her left hand and slipped it inside his dinnerjacket, pressing it against his chest so that through the thin material of his dress shirt she could feel the warmth of his body and the rapid beating of his heart.

'Don't think that because I haven't made a pass at you I haven't wanted to,' he said, looking into her eyes with a suddenly hungry light in his own. 'I have...many times. But I sensed you weren't ready for it, and I know from listening to my sisters comparing notes how often guys get written off because they go too fast too soon.'

'It's a pity all men don't have a trio of sisters to put them wise to the way women feel about things,' Maggie said, smiling.

She knew that, given the smallest sign of encouragement, he would forget about her lipstick and take her in his arms. Had she loved him, she wouldn't have cared about her make-up. To feel his lips on hers would have been the most important thing in the world.

Fortunately, from her point of view, at that moment someone in the hall called out, 'William... Maggie... where are you?'

William said something under his breath and reluctantly released her hands.

'Just having a quiet snifter away from the blast of rock,' he said, as they joined the rest of the party in the hall.

As Maggie hadn't had time to do more than sip her Campari and soda, and his glass was also almost full, it must have been clear to everyone that, even if they hadn't been locked in an ardent embrace, they hadn't been doing much drinking.

It was about two hours later, when the party was in full swing at the country house, that Dr Bramshott asked Maggie to dance with him.

'I'm afraid that so far my wife and I haven't had much chance to talk to you, my dear, but tomorrow should be a more leisurely day. William's told us a great deal about you. You're a very talented young woman and a successful one too, I gather.'

'Do you disapprove of career-women?' she asked. 'Or rather, of women who choose careers outside the home? Because obviously being a doctor's wife and the mother of five children is an extremely demanding career at which your wife has been extremely successful. One has only to look at you and your sons and daughters to see that.'

'Yes, Laura has been the ideal wife for a GP and, fortunately, it was what she wanted to be. I only disapprove of people being unhappy and frustrated as, in past generations, many women were,' he answered. 'Not that the greater opportunities they have today always bring contentment. I have an increasing number of female patients who are suffering from stress because their lives are too full of responsibilities. In many cases it's because their husbands aren't doing enough to help.'

Whether he was sounding her views, as they discussed this subject, and would later relay them to his wife, Maggie wasn't sure. She felt that the doctor and his family were all favourably disposed towards her, but would quickly change their good opinion if she kept William on a string.

That was not what she wanted to do, but was it right to commit herself while another man held her heart, even if her love for him could never have a happy outcome?

At ten o'clock a delicious fork supper was served and she was introduced to more of the Bramshotts' friends.

Then, after the hour-long supper break, another selection of music suitable for a gathering of all age groups was put on the cassette-player in the corner of the large room where the party was being held.

Maggie danced a fast number with Joey, the slit in her skirt flying open to show her black-stockinged legs.

'My turn,' said William, coming to claim her while she was catching her breath. With typical thoughtfulness, he had brought her a long soft drink.

'Just what I needed,' she said gratefully, draining the glass.

As she went into his arms, her cheeks flushed from the exertion of partnering his energetic young brother, a slower number was beginning. The opening strains were familiar, but it wasn't until the caressing tenor voice began singing that she realised it was one of Adam's big hits, 'Do you remember Babylon?'

It shouldn't have surprised her to hear him. She ought to have guessed that before the evening was over at least one of his songs would be played. It was just unfortunate that she happened to be dancing with William when it happened. They had danced together before supper, but not to the slow, sensuous beat of this kind of music.

Do you remember the fountains . . . the scent of roses . . . the moonlight?

Unaware of her anguish, William drew her closer, resting his cheek against her temple.

All night we made love . . . our last night together . . .

The tenderness with which Adam sang the lyrics he had written brought a great lump to Maggie's throat. Circling the floor in William's arms, surrounded by friendly people, she had never felt more isolated, more lonely.

Now . . . in the night . . . I dream that you're in my arms, Dreams are all I have left . . .

To her horror, Maggie's eyes filled with tears and she felt a sob rise in her throat.

Some inkling that all was not well had communicated itself to William. One glance at her face was enough to tell him that she was in urgent need of somewhere private. The next moment Maggie was being shepherded swiftly from the dance-floor.

The refuge he found for her was the lift. It was probably the only place in the hotel where two people who weren't staying there could be certain of being alone for a few minutes. And those few minutes were long enough for Maggie to regain control of herself.

'It was that song, wasn't it?' William said gently, offering her the handkerchief from the breast pocket of his dinner-jacket. 'It reminded you of him.'

Taken aback that he knew who it was she had loved and lost, she stared at him in startled silence, her throat still tight with tears.

'There used to be a song which rather broke me up too at one time,' said William. 'It was one of Mona's favourites. For a long time afterwards whenever I heard it I thought about her...about us. It wouldn't have that effect now.' He put an arm round her shoulders. 'You'll get over him, Maggie. Just give it time.'

'Shall I?' she said shakily. 'I wish I could believe that. Oh, William, I'm so sorry. I didn't mean to cast a blight on this happy evening. I should never have come down with you in the first place. It wasn't being fair. I haven't been fair to you at all.'

'Not true...nonsense,' he said positively. 'I knew right from the start that it wasn't going to be plain sailing for us. That first day Ted and I had lunch with you—remember?—I knew you'd been through a bad time. I thought probably there'd been a divorce or a long-term partnership which had broken up. Later Ted asked Alice about you, but she said that nobody knew anything about your love-life—if you had one. Look, I know you don't feel like dancing any more, so let's go for a walk. It's not cold out.'

But Maggie didn't think that was a good idea. Obviously, having confided his own youthful heartbreak to her, William would expect to be told what had gone wrong in her life, and the last thing she wanted was to talk about it.

Besides, if William discovered it was the singer as much as the song which had upset her, he wouldn't take her feelings seriously. He would think she was merely suffering from a foolish infatuation.

'No, no—that won't do at all. Your mother wouldn't like it if we disappeared from the party. I'll be all right now,' she insisted.

On the surface the rest of the weekend passed pleasantly and smoothly. Whether William said anything to Dr and Mrs Bramshott before she came down to breakfast, Maggie didn't know and didn't ask. But she sensed a subtle change in their manner towards her; the almost imperceptible difference between parents being nice to a future daughter-in-law and to a visiting girlfriend who might or might not join the family.

'I hope you'll come again, Maggie,' said Laura Bramshott, when they said goodbye after tea on Sunday afternoon.

But, as she and William drove back to London, Maggie knew it was her first and last visit to the house at Bath. The weekend had proved to her that, fond as she was of William, having known and loved Adam she could never be satisfied with a second-best relationship.

She remembered the French expression he had used to describe his own liaison with Elizabeth Vazon. *Faute de mieux*. For want of something better. No way would that do for her. If she couldn't have marriage to and children by the man she loved, she would settle for being a career-woman.

It was a more silent journey than the drive down. They talked of impersonal matters from time to time, but for much of the way William had the radio on while Maggie faced the bleak fact that she must stop having an out-of-office-hours friendship with him. It wasn't fair to continue a relationship which could never have the outcome he wanted.

Deep down she had known that all along, she thought guiltily, but had refused to face it because it would leave such a gap in her life.

On the outskirts of London, he said, 'Would you like to see the new Meryl Streep film later in the week?'

'I doubt if I shall have time for anything but work this week, William. I've been asked to write some articles on decorating for a women's magazine, and it's going to take up a lot of my time for the next month or two. You'll be extra busy too, I imagine, working on your new contract.'

'I don't think it's a good idea to take work home, as it were. You know what they say about all work and no play.'

'But in fact most people who get to the top in any sphere don't work a forty-hour week or anything like it. I shall have to work in the evenings to get these articles done.'

'Must you work on them *every* night?'

'I think I should.'

He was silent for a while. At last he said, 'Are you telling me we should see less of each other?'

'I think it would be wiser.'

'Oh, Maggie...' He gave a deep sigh. 'It would have been better if I'd kept my big mouth shut...given you more time to get over this other guy...damn and blast him.'

'I'm older than you and Mona were. I—I may never get over him,' she said, in a low voice.

It was a measure of William's character that he took one hand off the wheel, reached for her right hand and gave it a comforting squeeze.

Having delivered her to her door, he didn't insist on carrying her light case upstairs, but said goodbye at the street door.

'OK, we'll play it your way for a while,' he said, in an equable tone which didn't match the sadness in his eyes. 'Just remember, if you change your mind, I shall still be around.'

Unexpectedly, he leaned forward and kissed her, as he had meant to kiss her after the party last night but in the event had refrained.

In the middle of the following week Maggie was in her office when Alice came in to say, 'I've just opened the street door for Mrs Perelle, Adam Rocquaine's house-keeper. She's on her way up.'

'Mrs Perelle?' Momentarily Maggie looked blank. Then a hideous thought struck her.

She leapt from her chair and left the office like a whirlwind.

'Don't go and break *your* wrist,' Alice called after her.

The warning had no effect. Maggie tore down the staircase, meeting her visitor half-way up the second flight with the urgent demand, 'What's happened—what's happened to Adam?'

'There's nothing wrong. Don't be alarmed. Mr Adam is fine. Well, no...he's not fine...but he's in good health,' said his housekeeper. 'I'm sorry if I gave you a fright. The reason I'm here is that I'd like to talk to you, Miss Hornchurch. Have I come at an inconvenient time?'

'No, not at all. Let's go upstairs to my flat. How long are you staying in London?'

'Just for the day,' said the older woman. 'There was no fog this morning. I came over on the early flight and caught the bus from Heathrow to Marble Arch. From there I came by taxi. I'll go back on the last flight this evening. There are one or two bits of shopping I want to do this afternoon, but my main purpose in coming was to have a talk with you. Perhaps I'm interfering in something which is none of my business, but I feel I have to do something.'

'Something about what?' asked Maggie, showing her into the flat.

'About Mr Adam being so depressed. He tries to hide it, but I've known him a long time. I can tell he's in very low spirits. He hasn't been himself since you left the island, Miss Hornchurch. I don't know what happened between you, but I've a shrewd idea that Elizabeth Vazon managed to spoil things for the pair of you.'

'Let's sit down.' Maggie indicated the sofa where she and Adam had sat on his visit to the flat. 'Would you like a cup of tea, Mrs Perelle?'

'I would, indeed! I had one on the plane, but it wasn't very nice. I didn't have breakfast before I left home. There wasn't time. I didn't plan to come to London today, you see. It was an impulse...perhaps a foolish one. My husband used to tell me I was too impulsive.'

'I don't think an impulse to help people can ever be wrong,' said Maggie. 'Make yourself comfortable. I'll be back in a few minutes.'

Before she had finished making the tea, Mrs Perelle followed her to the kitchen. 'It's a very nice place you have here. Do you have a daily help?'

'No, I do my own cleaning and cooking.'

'You keep it beautifully,' said the other woman. 'I'm surprised you have the time.'

'It's just a matter of organising routines and sticking to them. A neat person, living alone, doesn't make a lot of housework.'

'That's something I never understood...how Mr Adam could put up with Elizabeth's untidy ways,' said Mrs Perelle. 'You may think it's not my place to speak my mind about her, Miss Hornchurch, but you have to understand that in Guernsey there aren't the same social distinctions as here on the mainland. It's a more equal society, where everyone expects to be treated with respect and a man's standing in the community doesn't depend on his work or the size of his house. Mrs Rocquaine never thought me her inferior because I worked for her. She often confided her worries to me, especially during her last months. She'd had a long, happy life. Her only regret was that she wouldn't live to see her grandson happily married.'

Maggie took the tray into the living-room.

'Mrs Rocquaine didn't like Elizabeth, I gather?'

'You can like a person in spite of their faults and weaknesses,' said Mrs Perelle. 'She didn't dislike Elizabeth when they were all growing up together. She was sorry for the girl for having no mother and being spoilt by her father. Mrs Rocquaine didn't worry when both Mr Adam and Mr Guy were in love with Elizabeth and she was flirting with them both, playing one off against the other. She said it was only calf love which the two boys would outgrow...as Mr Adam did. He realised a long time ago there wasn't much to Elizabeth except her looks and her liking for a good time.'

'That isn't what she told me when she came to see me at the hotel,' said Maggie. 'She said they belonged to-gether...always had and always would.'

'That girl would go to any lengths to get her own way!' Mrs Perelle exclaimed crossly. 'She's been determined to have him since she was in her teens, and it doesn't matter a jot that he doesn't want to marry her. What she's set her heart on, she'll have. She's as stubborn as they come. You shouldn't have believed whatever nonsense she told you, Miss Hornchurch. Of course Mr Adam wouldn't say much against her. That's not his way. He wouldn't feel it was right to tell anyone what a nuisance she's been to him. She's a lovely-looking girl and she can be very kind and very sweet when she wants to be. But, oh, dear, if somebody thwarts her, she can be a real menace.'

She paused to stir her tea. 'If you let Elizabeth stand between you and Mr Adam—I know how much he cares for you, and it was my impression you felt the same about him—you'll be missing a great deal of happiness with someone who's as good and true as they come. He'll make a wonderful husband for the right girl...and it's my belief you are the right girl for him,' she added with conviction.

'Where is Adam now?' asked Maggie.

'He's here in London. He came over yesterday. When he rang me up last night, I hoped to hear he'd come to see you. But you know the old saying...if the mountain won't come to Mahomet, Mahomet must go to the mountain. I know he's busy with various meetings today, but why don't you see him tonight, after the show?'

'What show?'

'He's on TV this evening.'

The chat-show presenter was a woman. Her first guest was a sedate-looking woman who had just won the Golden Dagger award for the best crime novel of the year. She was followed by an American fashion designer to whom, in any other circumstances, Maggie would have listened with interest. Tonight she sat through the interview in a fever of impatience, listening but not hearing.

At last the designer was thanked for coming on the show and the presenter turned to look into the eye of the camera.

'My last guest is someone I've always wanted to meet, and I know most of the ladies in the audience, and at home, would love to change places with me tonight. Before he joins me, he's going to sing his latest song. Ladies and gentlemen—Adam Rocquaine.'

To uproarious applause, shouts and whistles from the studio audience, another camera panned in to a dais at the back of the stage where a small orchestra was waiting to accompany Adam.

Maggie remembered Alice saying that he never mimed, nor did his songs have fade-out endings.

The camera and a bright spotlight focused on a curtained entrance behind the musicians.

Then Adam stepped into the beam of light and the clapping and cheering redoubled as he made his way to the mike at the front of the dais. He bowed but he didn't smile. After raising his hand in a gesture which both acknowledged the applause and stilled it, he unclipped the mike from its stand and held it in his right hand, his eyes glinting like sapphires as he gave the now hushed and expectant audience a curiously sombre stare.

'We are not strangers, you and I...not since that night at Bella's Place...'

Maggie caught her breath. She had a vivid memory of Laurian Thornham's dinner, and Adam asking her if she had been involved with William before she went to Barbados. 'Has it suddenly become the thing to ask personal questions?' she had asked him haughtily.

'You and I are not strangers, Maggie.'

His reply had disturbed her at the time. To find he had used it in a song—a song about their first evening together—was shattering.

There were tears in her eyes long before the song ended, tears which brimmed over and slid down her cheeks as she watched Adam replace the mike and bow to the wild applause. Then he stepped down from the dais and strode briskly across the stage to the area where the presenter was also clapping enthusiastically.

Instead of kissing her cheek, as the designer had, Adam chose the more appropriate gesture of kissing her hand.

'That really is a beautiful song, Adam,' she said, as they sat down. 'Judging by our audience's reaction, it's going to be another big hit for you. Tell me, is Bella's Place imaginary? Or does it really exist?'

Although Adam looked as relaxed as if they were chatting in private, there was something about him which had changed since the last time Maggie saw him. She realised what it was. So far he hadn't smiled.

'It exists . . . but I won't tell you where,' he answered. 'If too many people discovered it, it might change from the way it is . . . the way I like it.'

'This new song is rather sad. In fact, most of your songs have a vein of sadness running through them. In "Do You Remember Babylon?" the lovers were torn apart. In "Bella's Place" they meet but she goes away. Is this how you see love . . . as happiness followed by heartbreak?'

'No, I wouldn't say that. In my observation, people who truly love each other tend to stay together . . . to be "happy ever after" as the old storybooks used to say. But it can take a long time to find the right person, and sometimes when people do find each other there are circumstances which create difficulties.'

'You're not married, are you, Adam? Is that because you haven't met the right girl yet?' she asked rather coquettishly. It was plain that she fancied him.

A faint glimmer of his customary charm showed through the unusual gravity of his manner tonight. 'I frequently meet very charming and attractive women,' he replied, with a trace of a smile. 'But there's only one girl I want to marry.'

'May we know who she is?'

He shook his head. 'But I will tell you that "Bella's Place" was written for her and when she hears it . . . if she hears it . . . I hope she'll know'—he turned, looking straight into the lens of the camera so that he seemed to be looking into Maggie's eyes—'how much I miss her and need her.'

'How intriguing,' said his hostess. 'Unfortunately there isn't time to ask you why she isn't with you now. However, I'm quite sure this mysterious woman in your life can't fail to hear "Bella's Place". Congratulations on another hit, Adam, and thank you for singing it for us, whoever inspired it. She's a lucky girl, wouldn't you say, ladies?'

There was a roar of agreement.

In the taxi to his flat, Maggie wondered if she ought to have telephoned the BBC and tried to get an urgent message to him.

For all she knew, he might be going out to dinner after the show and wouldn't return to his flat until late. But it didn't matter how long she had to wait. She had to see him tonight. The song he had written for her had erased the last doubt in her mind that, whatever Elizabeth might have been to him in the past, she was not the one he loved now.

Adam's London address proved to be a tall neo-Georgian building in the heart of Mayfair. A revolving door gave a glimpse of an elegant ground-floor lobby.

As she entered, a liveried porter rose from a desk by the entrance where he had been reading a newspaper.

'Good evening, miss.'

'Good evening. I've come to see Mr Rocquaine.'

'Is he expecting you, miss?' The man's rather wary expression made her realise he might suspect her of being a fan of Adam's who had somehow found out where he lived and who might make a nuisance of herself.

'No, but I'm sure he'll see me...when he gets back. I know he was on television tonight.' To establish that she was *bona fide* she added, 'My name is Maggie Hornchurch. I'm an interior designer. Earlier this year I was working on a house for Mr Rocquaine.'

As soon as she said who she was, the porter's guarded manner changed.

'Mr Rocquaine was hoping you might call, Miss Hornchurch. He left instructions that he was to be contacted immediately if you called or telephoned. As a matter of fact he got back from the studio a couple of minutes before you arrived. This way, please.'

He led her to the lift and pressed the button. 'My wife was going to video the show for me to watch later. Did you see it yourself?'

'Yes, I did. Mr Rocquaine sang a new song he's composed.'

Maggie had left her flat in great haste, pausing to grab a raincoat and her bag, but not to do her face or hair.

She wondered suddenly if the tears she had shed while Adam was singing had left marks on her face. But the porter didn't seem to notice anything strange about her appearance.

'Top floor... flat number two... to your right as you leave the lift,' he said, when the door slid open.

Less than a minute later she was pressing the bell beside Adam's front door, her heart beating like a pile-driver.

When he opened the door he was frowning as if it hadn't pleased him to be disturbed so soon after his return.

'Maggie!' he exclaimed, startled. 'What brings you here?'

'I heard you sing "Bella's Place" on television. How could I not come?' she said, with a tremor in her voice. 'It was me you were talking about, wasn't it?'

Adam gave an odd, shaken laugh. 'It was you. Oh Maggie, my love...'

He swept her into his arms and crushed her to him.

It was some time before either of them was sufficiently recovered from the joy of being reunited to be able to talk in more than disjointed murmurs between kisses.

By that stage they were no longer locked in a passionate embrace on the threshold, but were closely entwined on the sofa in Adam's living-room.

'I have never regretted anything more than that letter, but when I wrote it I was angry that you had so little faith in me,' he told her. 'You have to realise, my darling, that behind the public image there is a real human being with all the faults and frailties that human beings have. I wanted you to believe in me without question; to be on my side in everything; to trust me no matter how damning the evidence against me.'

'I should never have doubted you—not for one moment,' she agreed. 'But my head kept saying to my heart: can you believe that this marvellous man is really mad about someone as ordinary as *you*? The fact is, I have a lot of confidence in myself as a designer, but not very much in myself as a woman.'

'Goodness knows why not when you're such an adorable one. Tomorrow I was going to come and see you—to apologise for that insufferable letter and to try to make you believe that whatever Elizabeth said to you wasn't true... as one day she may admit.'

'I do believe that now,' said Maggie. 'I was a fool to be influenced by her. Oh, Adam, I've been so miserable since I left the island. I couldn't believe my ears when you started to sing "Bella's Place".'

'All my songs have been written for you,' he told her softly. 'Even before we met, you were my inspiration, Maggie. That's why I have the feeling that my best songs have yet to be written; and from now on they won't be songs about searching for love. They'll be about finding it.'

Harlequin Presents®

Coming Next Month

Available in June wherever paperback books are sold, or through Harlequin Reader Service:

In the U.S.
901 Fuhrmann Blvd.
P.O. Box 1397
Buffalo, N.Y. 14240-1397

In Canada
P.O. Box 603
Fort Erie, Ontario
L2A 5X3

Indulge a Little
Give a Lot

A LITTLE SELF-INDULGENCE CAN DO A WORLD OF GOOD!

Last fall readers indulged themselves with fine romance and free gifts during the Harlequin®/ Silhouette® "Indulge A Little—Give A Lot" promotion. For every specially marked book purchased, 5¢ was donated by Harlequin/ Silhouette to Big Brothers/Big Sisters Programs and Services in the United States and Canada. We are pleased to announce that your participation in this unique promotion resulted in a total contribution of *$100,000.*

*

Watch for details on Harlequin® and Silhouette®'s next exciting promotion in September.

THE LOVES OF A CENTURY...

Join American Romance in a nostalgic look back at the Twentieth Century—at the lives and loves of American men and women from the turn-of-the-century to the dawn of the year 2000.

Journey through the decades from the dance halls of the 1900s to the discos of the seventies ... from Glenn Miller to the Beatles ... from Valentino to Newman ... from corset to miniskirt ... from beau to Significant Other.

Relive the moments ... recapture the memories.

Look for the CENTURY OF AMERICAN ROMANCE series starting next month in Harlequin American Romance. In one of the four American Romance titles appearing each month, for the next twelve months, we'll take you back to a decade of the Twentieth Century, where you'll relive the years and rekindle the romance of days gone by.

Don't miss a day of the CENTURY OF AMERICAN ROMANCE.

The women...the men...the passions...
the memories....

CARM-1

Have You Ever Wondered If You Could Write A Harlequin Novel?

Here's great news—Harlequin is offering a series of cassette tapes to help you do just that. Written by Harlequin editors, these tapes give practical advice on how to make your characters—and your story— come alive. There's a tape for each contemporary romance series Harlequin publishes.

Mail order only

All sales final

TO: *Harlequin Reader Service*
Audiocassette Tape Offer
P.O. Box 1396
Buffalo, NY 14269-1396

I enclose a check/money order payable to HARLEQUIN READER SERVICE® for $9.70 ($8.95 plus 75¢ postage and handling) for EACH tape ordered for the total sum of $_____*
Please send:

☐ Romance and Presents   ☐ Intrigue
☐ American Romance   ☐ Temptation
☐ Superromance   ☐ All five tapes ($38.80 total)

Signature_____
                                              (please print clearly)
Name:_____
Address:_____
State:_____ Zip:_____
*Iowa and New York residents add appropriate sales tax.   **AUDIO-H**

Harlequin Regency Romance™

Romance the way it was *always* meant to be!

The time is 1811, when a Regent Prince rules the empire. The place is London, the glittering capital where rakish dukes and dazzling debutantes scheme and flirt in a dangerously exciting game. Where marriage is the passport to wealth and power, yet every girl hopes secretly for love....

Welcome to Harlequin Regency Romance where reading is an adventure and romance is *not* just a thing of the past! Two delightful books a month.

Available wherever Harlequin Books are sold.

REG-1R